CHILDREN'S
CLASSICS

THE MAN IN THE IRON MASK

Alexandre Dumas

Bloomsbury Books
London

This edition published 1994 by Bloomsbury Books, an imprint of The Godfrey Cave Group, 42 Bloomsbury Street, London, WC1B 3QJ.

ISBN 1 85471 295 0

Printed and bound by Firmin-Didot (France), Group Herissey. No d'impression : 26506.

Contents

1

Three Guests Astonished To Find Themselves At Supper Together

The carriage arrived at the outside gate of the Bastille. A soldier on guard stopped it, but d'Artagnan had only to utter a single word to procure admittance, and the carriage passed on without further difficulty. Whilst they were proceeding along the covered way which led to the courtyard of the governor's residence, d'Artagnan, whose lynx eye saw everything, even through the walls, suddenly cried out, "What is that out yonder?"

"Well," said Athos quietly, "what is it?"

"Look yonder, Athos."

"In the courtyard?"

"Why, yes; make haste."

"Well, a carriage; very likely conveying a prisoner like myself."

"That would be too droll."

"I do not understand you."

"Make haste and look again, and look at the man who is just getting out of that carriage."

At that very moment a second sentinel stopped d'Artagnan, and while the formalities were being gone through, Athos could see at a hundred paces from him the man whom his friend had pointed out to him. He was, in fact, getting out of the carriage at the door of the governor's house. "Well," inquired d'Artagnan, "do you see him?"

"Yes; he is a man in a grey suit."

"What do you say of him?"

"I cannot very well tell; he is, as I have just told you, a man in a grey suit, who is getting out of a carriage; that is all."

"Athos, I will wager anything it is he."

"He—who?"

"Aramis."

"Aramis arrested? Impossible!"

"I do not say he is arrested, since we see him alone in his carriage."

"Well, then, what is he doing here?"

"Oh, he knows Baisemeaux, the governor," replied the musketeer slyly; "so we have arrived just in time."

"What for?"

"In order to see what we can see."

"I regret this meeting exceedingly. When Aramis sees me, he will be very much annoyed, in the first place at seeing me, and in the next at being seen."

"Very well reasoned."

"Unfortunately, there is no remedy for it; whenever any one meets another in the Bastille, even if he wished to draw back to avoid him, it would be impossible."

"Athos, I have an idea; the question is, to spare Aramis the annoyance you were speaking of, is it not?"

"What is to be done?"

"I will tell you; or, in order to explain myself in the best possible way, let me relate the affair in my own manner; I will not recommend you to tell a falsehood, for that would be impossible for you to do; but I will tell falsehoods enough for both; it is so easy to do that with the nature and habits of a Gascon."

Athos smiled. The carriage stopped where the one we have just now pointed out had stopped; namely, at the door of the governor's house. "It is understood, then?" said d'Artagnan, in a low voice to his friend. Athos consented by a gesture. They ascended the staircase. There will be no occasion for surprise at the facility with which they had entered into the Bastille, if it be remembered that, before passing the first gate, in fact, the most difficult of all, d'Artagnan had announced that he had brought a prisoner of state. At the third gate, on the contrary, that is to say, when he had once fairly entered the prison, he merely said to the sentinel, "To M. Baisemeaux;" and they both passed on. In a few minutes they were in the governor's dining-room, and the first face which attracted d'Artagnan's observation was that of Aramis, who was seated side by side with Baisemeaux, and awaited the announcement of a good meal, whose odour impregnated the whole apartment. If d'Artagnan pretended surprise, Aramis did not pretend at all; he started when he saw his two friends, and his emotion was very apparent. Athos and d'Artagnan, however, compliment-ed him as usual, and Baisemeaux, amazed, completely stupe-fied by the presence of his three guests, began to perform a few evolutions around them all. "By what lucky accident—"

"We were just going to ask you," retorted d'Artagnan.

"Are we going to give ourselves up as prisoners?" cried Aramis, with an affectation of hilarity.

"Ah! ah!" said d'Artagnan; "it is true the walls smell deu-cedly like a prison. Monsieur de Baisemeaux, you know you invited me to sup with you the other day."

"I!" cried Baisemeaux.

"Yes, of course you did, although you now seem so struck with amazement. Don"t you remember it?"

"Yes, yes; you're quite right; how could I have forgotten; I remember it now as well as possible; I beg you a thousand pardons. But now, once for all, my dear M. d'Artagnan, be sure that at this present time, as at any other, whether invit-ed or not, you are perfectly at home here, you and M. d'Herblay, your friend," he said, turning towards Aramis; "and this gentleman too," he added, bowing to Athos.

"Well, I thought it would be sure to turn out so," replied d'Artagnan, "and that is the reason I came. Having nothing to do this evening at the Palais-Royal, I wished to judge for myself what your ordinary style of living was like; and as I was coming alone, I met the Comte de la Fère." He presented Athos who bowed. "The Comte, who had just left His Majesty, handed me an order which required immediate attention. We were close by here; I wished to call in, even if it were for no other object than that of shaking hands with you and of presenting the Comte to you, of whom you spoke so highly that evening at the palace when—"

"Certainly, certainly,—M. le Comte de la Fère."

"Precisely."

"The Comte is welcome, I am sure."

"And he will sup with you two, I suppose, whilst I, unfortunate dog that I am, must run off on a matter of duty. Oh! what happy beings you are, compared to myself," he added, sighing as loud as Porthos might have done.

"And so you are going away then?" said Aramis and Baisemeaux together, with the same expression of delighted surprise, the tone of which was immediately noticed by d'Artagnan.

"I leave you in my place," he said, "a noble and excellent guest." And he touched Athos gently on the shoulder, who, astonished also, could not prevent exhibiting his surprise a little; a tone which was noticed by Aramis only, for M. de Baisemeaux was not quite equal to the three friends in point of intelligence.

"What! Are you going to leave us?" resumed the governor.

"I shall only be about an hour, or an hour and a half. I will return in time for dessert."

"Oh, we will wait for you," said Baisemeaux.

"No, no; that would be really disobliging me."

"You will be sure to return, though?" said Athos, with an expression of doubt.

"Most certainly," he said, pressing his friend's hand confidently; and he added in a low voice, "Wait for me, Athos; be cheerful and lively as possible, and above all, don't allude even to business affairs, for Heaven's sake."

And with a renewed pressure of the hand, he seemed to warn the Comte of the necessity of keeping perfectly discreet and impenetrable. Baisemeaux led d'Artagnan to the gate. Aramis, with many friendly protestations of delight, sat down by Athos, determined to make him speak; but Athos possessed every virtue and quality to the very highest degree. If necessity had required it, he would have been the finest orator in the world, but on other occasions he would rather have died than have opened his lips.

Ten minutes after d'Artagnan's departure, the three gentlemen sat down to table, which was covered with the most substantial display of gastronomic luxury. Large joints, exquisite dishes, preserves, the greatest variety of wines, appeared successively upon the table, which was served at the King's expense. Baisemeaux was the only one who ate and drank resolutely. Aramis allowed nothing to pass by him, but merely touched everything he took; Athos, after the soup, and three *hors d'œuvres*, ate nothing more. The style of conversation was such as could hardly be otherwise between three men so opposite in temper and ideas. Aramis was incessantly asking himself by what extraordinary chance Athos was at Baisemeaux's when d'Artagnan was no longer there, and why d'Artagnan did not remain when Athos was there. Athos sounded all the depths of the mind of Aramis, who lived in the midst of subterfuge, evasion and intrigue; he studied his man well and thoroughly, and felt convinced that he was engaged upon some important project. And then he, too, began to think of his own personal affair, and to lose himself in conjectures as to d'Artagnan's reason for having left the Bastille so abruptly, and for leaving behind him a prisoner so badly introduced and so badly looked after by the prison authorities. But we shall not pause to examine into the thoughts and feelings of these personages, but will leave them to themselves, surrounded by the remains of poultry, game, and fish, which Baisemeaux's generous knife and fork had so mutilated.

2

Political Rivals

D'Artagnan had promised M. de Baisemeaux to return in time for dessert, and he kept his word. They had just reached the finer and more delicate class of wines and liqueurs with which the governor's cellar had the reputation of being most admirably stocked, when the spurs of the captain resounded in the corridor, and he himself appeared at the threshold. Athos and Aramis had played a close game; neither of the two had been able to gain the slightest advantage over the other. They had supped, talked a good deal about the Bastille, of the last journey to Fontainebleau, of the intended fête that M. Fouquet, Superintendent of Finances, was about to give at Vaux in honour of the King; they had generalised on every possible subject; and no one, excepting Baisemeaux, had, in the slightest degree, alluded to private matters. D'Artagnan arrived in the very midst of the conversation, pale and much disturbed. Baisemeaux hastened to give him a chair; d'Artagnan accepted a glass of wine, and set it down empty. Athos and Aramis both remarked his emotion; as for Baisemeaux, he saw nothing more than the captain of the King's musketeers, to whom he endeavoured to show every possible attention. But, although Aramis had remarked his emotion, he had not been able to guess the cause of it. Athos alone believed he had detected it. For him, d'Artagnan's return, and particularly the manner in which he, usually so impassive, seemed overcome, signified, "I have just asked the King something which the King has refused me." Thoroughly convinced that his conjecture was correct, Athos smiled, rose from the table, and made a sign to d'Artagnan as if to remind him that they had something else to do than to sup together. D'Artagnan immediately understood him, and replied by another sign. Aramis and Baisemeaux watched this silent dialogue, and looked inquiringly at each other. Athos felt that he was called upon to give an explanation of what was passing.

"The truth is, my friends," said the Comte de la Fère, with a smile, "that you, Aramis, have been supping with a state criminal, and you, Monsieur de Baisemeaux, with your prisoner."

Baisemeaux uttered an exclamation of surprise, and almost of delight; for he was exceedingly proud and vain of his fortress; and, for his own individual profit, the more prisoners he had, the happier he was; and the higher the prisoners were in rank, the prouder he felt. Aramis assumed an expression of countenance which he thought the position justified, and said, "Well, dear Athos, forgive me; but I almost suspected what has happened. Some prank of your son, Raoul, and La Vallière, I suppose?"

"Alas!" said Baisemeaux.

"And," continued Aramis, "you, a high and powerful nobleman as you are, forgetful that courtiers now exist,—you have been to the King, I suppose, and told him what you thought of his conduct."

"Yes, you have guessed right."

"So that," said Baisemeaux, trembling at having supped so familiarly with a man who had fallen into disgrace with the King; "so that, Monsieur le Comte—"

"So that, my dear governor," said Athos, "my friend d'Artagnan will communicate to you the contents of the paper which I perceive just peeping out of his belt, and which assuredly can be nothing else than the order for my incarceration."

Baisemeaux held out his hand with his accustomed eagerness. D'Artagnan drew two papers from his belt, and presented one of them to the governor, who unfolded it, and then read, in a low tone of voice, looking at Athos over the paper, as he did so, and pausing from time to time: "'Order to detain in my château of the Bastille, Monsieur le Comte de la Fère.' Oh, monsieur, this is indeed a very melancholy honour for me."

"You will have a patient prisoner, monsieur," said Athos, in his calm, soft voice.

"A prisoner, too, who will not remain a month with you, my dear governor," said Aramis; while Baisemeaux, still holding the order in his hand, transcribed it upon the prison registry.

"Not a day, or rather not even a night," said d'Artagnan, displaying the second order of the King, "for now, dear M. de Baisemeaux, you will have the goodness to transcribe also this order for setting the Comte immediately at liberty."

"Ah!" said Aramis, "it is a labour that you have deprived me of, d'Artagnan;" and he pressed the musketeer's hand in a significant manner, at the same moment as that of Athos.

"What!" said the latter, in astonishment. "The King sets me at liberty!"

"Read, my dear friend," returned d'Artagnan.

Athos took the order and read it. "It is quite true," he said.

"Are you sorry for it?" asked d'Artagnan.

"Oh, no, on the contrary; I wish the King no harm; and the greatest evil or misfortune that anyone can wish Kings, is that they should commit an act of injustice. But you have had a difficult and painful task, I know. Tell me, have you not, d'Artagnan?"

"I? Not at all," said the musketeer, laughing; "the King does everything I wish him to do."

Aramis looked fixedly at d'Artagnan, and saw that he was not speaking the truth. But Baisemeaux had eyes for nothing but d'Artagnan, so great was his admiration for a man who seemed to make the King do all he wished. "And does the King exile Athos?" inquired Aramis.

"No, not precisely; the King did not explain himself upon that subject," replied d'Artagnan; "but I think the Comte could not well do better, unless, indeed, he wishes particularly to thank the King—"

"No, indeed," replied Athos, smiling.

"Well, then, I think," resumed d'Artagnan, "that the Comte cannot do better than return to his own château. However, my dear Athos, you have only to speak, to tell me what you want. If any particular place of residence is more agreeable to you than another, I am influential enough, perhaps, to obtain it for you."

"No, thank you," said Athos; "nothing can be more agreeable to me, my dear friend, than to return to my solitude beneath my noble trees, on the banks of the Loire. If Heaven be the overruling physician of the evils of the mind, nature is the sovereign remedy. And so, monsieur," continued Athos, turning again towards Baisemeaux, "I am now free, I suppose?"

"Yes, Monsieur le Comte, I think so—at least, I hope so," said the governor, turning over and over the two papers in question, "unless, however, M. d'Artagnan has a third order to give me."

"No, my dear Monsieur Baisemeaux, no," said the musketeer; "the second is quite enough; we can stop there."

"Ah! Monsieur le Comte," said Baisemeaux, addressing Athos, "you do not know what you are losing. I should have placed you among the thirty-franc prisoners, like the generals—what am I saying?—I mean among the fifty-franc, like the princes; and you would have supped every evening as you have done tonight."

"Allow me, monsieur," said Athos, "to prefer my own simpler fare." And then, turning to d'Artagnan, he said, "Let us go, my dear friend. Shall I have that greatest of all pleasures for me—that of having you as my companion?"

"To the city gate only," replied d'Artagnan, "after which I will tell you what I told the King. I am on duty."

"And you, my dear Aramis," said Athos, smiling; "will you accompany me?"

"Thank you, my dear friend," said Aramis, "but I have an appointment in Paris this evening, and I cannot leave without very serious interests suffering by my absence."

"In that case," said Athos, "I must say *adieu*, and take my leave of you. My dear Monsieur de Baisemeaux, I have to thank you exceedingly for your kind and friendly disposition towards me, and particularly for the specimen you have given me of the usual fare of the Bastille." And, having embraced Aramis, and shaken hands with M. de Baisemeaux, and having received their wishes for an agreeable journey from them both, Athos set off with d'Artagnan.

3

M. De Baisemeaux's "Society"

On quitting the Bastille, d'Artagnan and the Comte de la Fère left Aramis in close confabulation with Baisemeaux. When once these two guests had departed, Baisemeaux did not in the least perceive that the conversation suffered by their absence. The conversation, however, without flagging in appearance, flagged in reality; for Baisemeaux not only had it nearly all to himself, but further, kept speaking only of that singular event—the incarceration of Athos—followed by so prompt an order to set him again at liberty. Nor, moreover, had Baisemeaux failed to observe that the two orders, of arrest and of liberation, were both in the King's hand. But then, the King would not take the trouble to write similar orders except under pressing circumstances. All this was very interesting, and, above all, very puzzling to Baisemeaux; but as, on the other hand, all this was very clear to Aramis, the latter did not attach to the occurrence the same importance as did the worthy governor. Besides, Aramis rarely put himself out of the way for anything, and he had not yet told M. de Baisemeaux for what reason he had now done so. And so at the very climax of Baisemeaux's dissertation, Aramis suddenly interrupted him.

"Tell me, my dear M. Baisemeaux," said he, "have you never any other diversions at the Bastille than those at which I assisted during the two or three visits I have had the honour to pay you?"

This address was so unexpected that the governor

was quite dumbfounded at it. "Diversions," said he, "but I take them continually, monseigneur."

"Visits, no doubt?"

"No, not visits. Visits are not frequent at the Bastille."

"What, are visits rare, then?"

"Very much so."

"Even on the part of your society?"

"What do you term by my society—the prisoners?"

"Oh, no!—your prisoners, indeed! I know well it is you who visit them, and not they you. By your society I mean, my dear de Baisemeaux, the society of which you are a member."

Baisemeaux looked fixedly at Aramis, and then, as if the idea which had flashed across his mind were impossible, "Oh!" he said, "I have very little society at present. If I must own it to you, dear M. d'Herblay, the fact is, to stay at the Bastille appears, for the most part, distressing and distasteful to persons of the gay world."

"No, you don"t understand me, my dear M. Baisemeaux; you don"t understand me. I do not at all mean to speak of society in general, but of a particular society—of *the* society, in a word,—to which you are affiliated."

Baisemeaux nearly dropped the glass of muscat which he was in the act of raising to his lips. "Affiliated!" cried he, "affiliated!"

"Yes, affiliated, undoubtedly," repeated Aramis, with the greatest self-possession. "Are you not a member of a secret society, my dear M. Baisemeaux?"

"Secret?"

"Secret or mysterious."

"No, no; not the least in the world; no."

"Well," resumed Aramis, "if I say you are not a member of a secret or mysterious society, which you like to call it, the epithet is of no consequence; if I say you are not a member of a society similar to that I wish to designate, well, then, you will not understand a word of what I am going to say, that is all."

"Oh, be sure, beforehand, that I shall not understand any-thing."

"If, on the contrary, you are one of the members of this society, you will immediately answer me,— yes, or no."

"Begin your questions," continued Baisemeaux, trembling.

"You will agree, dear Monsieur de Baisemeaux," continued Aramis, with the same impassibility, "that it is evident a man cannot be a member of a society, it is evident that he cannot enjoy the advantages it offers to the affiliated, without being himself bound to certain little services."

"In short," stammered Baisemeaux, "that would be intelligible, if—"

"Well," resumed Aramis, "there is in the society of which I speak, and of which, as it seems, you are not a member—"

"Allow me," said Baisemeaux, "I should not like to say absolutely."

"There is an engagement entered into by all the governors and captains of fortresses affiliated to the order." Baisemeaux grew pale.

"Now the engagement," continued Aramis firmly, "is of this nature."

Baisemeaux rose, manifesting unspeakable emotion; "Go on, dear M. d'"Herblay; go on," he said.

Aramis then spoke, or rather recited the following paragraph in the same tone as if he had been reading it from a book. "The aforesaid captain or governor of a fortress shall allow to enter, when need shall arise, and on demand of the prisoner, a confessor affiliated to the order." He stopped. Baisemeaux was quite distressing to look at, being so wretchedly pale and trembling. "Is not that the text of the agreement?" quietly asked Aramis.

"Monseigneur!" began Baisemeaux.

"Ah, well, you begin to understand, I think."

"Monseigneur," cried Baisemeaux, "do not trifle with my unhappy mind! I find myself nothing in your hands, if you have the malignant desire to draw from me the little secrets of my administration."

"Oh, by no means; pray undeceive yourself, dear M. Baisemeaux; it is not the little secrets of your administration, but those of your conscience that I aim at."

"Well, then, my conscience be it, dear M. d'Herblay. But have some consideration for the situation I am in, which is no ordinary one."

"It is no ordinary one, my dear monsieur," continued the inflexible Aramis, "if you are a member of this society; but it is quite a natural one if free from all engagements. You are answerable only to the King."

"Well, monsieur, I obey only the King, and whom else would you have a French nobleman obey?"

Aramis did not yield an inch; but with that silvery voice of his, continued, "It is very pleasant," said he, "for a French nobleman, for a prelate of France, to hear a man of your mark express himself so loyally, dear de Baisemeaux, and having heard you, to believe no more than you do."

"Have you doubted, monsieur?"

"I? Oh, no!"

"And so you doubt no longer?"

"I have no longer any doubt that such a man as you, monsieur," said Aramis gravely, "does not faithfully serve the masters whom he voluntarily chose for himself."

"Masters!" cried Baisemeaux.

"Yes, masters I said."

"Monsieur d'Herblay, you are still jesting, are you not?"

"Oh, yes! I understand that it is a more difficult position to have several masters than one; but the embarrassment is owing to you, my dear Baisemeaux, and I am not the cause of it."

"Certainly not," returned the unfortunate governor, more embarrassed than ever; "but what are you doing? Are you going?"

"Yes, I am going."

"But you are behaving very strangely towards me, mon-seigneur."

"I am behaving strangely,—how do you make that out?"

"Have you sworn, then, to put me to the torture?"

"No, I should be sorry to do so."

"Remain then."

"I cannot. I have no longer anything to do here; and, in-deed, I have duties to fulfil elsewhere."

"Duties, so late as this?"

"Yes; understand me now, my dear de Baisemeaux. They told me at the place whence I came, "The aforesaid governor or captain will allow to enter, as need shall arise, on the prison-er's demand, a confessor affiliated with the order." I came; you do not know what I mean, and so I shall return to tell them that they are mistaken, and that they must send me elsewhere."

"What! You are—" cried Baisemeaux, looking at Aramis almost in terror.

"The confessor affiliated to the order," said Aramis, with-out changing his voice.

But, gentle as the words were, they had the same effect on the unhappy governor as a clap of thunder. Baisemeaux became livid, and it seemed to him as if Aramis's beaming eyes were two forks of flame, piercing to the very bottom of his soul. "The confessor!" murmured he; "you, monsei-gneur, Bishop of Vannes, the confessor to the order!"

"Yes, I; but we have nothing to unravel together, seeing that you are not one of the affiliated."

"Monseigneur!"

"And I understand that, not being so, you refuse to com-ply with its demands."

"Monseigneur, I do not say that I have nothing to do with the society."

"Ah, ah!"

"I say not that I refuse to obey."

"Nevertheless, M. de Baisemeaux, what has passed wears very much the air of resistance."

"Oh, no, monseigneur, no! I only wished to be certain."

"To be certain of what?" said Aramis, in a tone of supreme contempt.

"Of nothing at all, monseigneur." Baisemeaux lowered his voice and, bending before the prelate, said, "I am at all times and in all places at the disposal of my masters, but—"

"Very good. I like you better thus, monsieur," said Aramis, as he resumed his seat, and put out his glass to Baisemeaux, whose hand trembled so that he could not fill it. "You were saying 'but'—" continued Aramis.

"But," replied the unhappy man, "having no notice, I was far from expecting."

"Does not the Gospel say, 'Watch, for the moment is known only of God.' Do not the rules of the order say, 'Watch, for that which I will you ought always to will also.' And on what pretext is it that you did not expect the confessor, M. de Baisemeaux?"

"Because, monseigneur, there is at present in the Bastille no prisoner ill."

Aramis shrugged his shoulders, "What do you know about that?" said he.

"But, nevertheless, it appears to me—"

"M. de Baisemeaux," said Aramis, turning round in his chair, "here is your servant, who wishes to speak with you;" and, at this moment, de Baisemeaux's servant appeared at the threshold of the door.

"What is it?" asked Baisemeaux sharply.

"Monsieur," said the man, "they are bringing you the doctor's return."

Aramis looked at Baisemeaux with a calm and confident eye.

"Well," said he, "let the messenger enter."

The messenger entered, saluted, and handed in the report. Baisemeaux ran his eye over it, and raising his head said, in surprise, "No.12 is ill."

"How was it then," said Aramis carelessly, "that you told me everybody was well in your hotel, M. de Baisemeaux?"

The governor then made a sign to the messenger, and when he had quitted the room said, still trembling, "I think there is in the article, 'on the prisoner's demand.'"

"Yes, it is so," answered Aramis. "But see what it is they want with you now."

At that moment, a sergeant put his head in at the door. "What do you want now?" cried Baisemeaux. "Can you not leave me in peace for ten minutes?"

"Monsieur," said the sergeant, "the sick man, No. 12, has commissioned the turnkey to request you to send him a confessor."

Baisemeaux very nearly sank on the floor; but Aramis disdained to reassure him, just as he had disdained to terrify him. "What must I answer?" inquired Baisemeaux.

"Just what you please," replied Aramis, compressing his lips; "that is your business. *I* am not governor of the Bastille."

"Tell the prisoner," cried Baisemeaux quickly— "tell the prisoner that his request is granted." The sergeant left the room. "Oh, monseigneur, monseigneur," murmured Baisemeaux, "how could I have suspected? How could I have foreseen this?"

"Who requested you to suspect, and who besought you to foresee?" contemptuously answered Aramis. "The order suspects; the order knows; the order foresees—is not that enough?"

"What do you command?" added Baisemeaux.

"I?—nothing at all. I am nothing but a poor priest, a simple confessor. Have I your orders to go and see the sufferer?"

"Oh, monseigneur, I do not order; I pray you to go."

"'Tis well; then conduct me to him."

4

The Prisoner

Since Aramis's singular transformation into a confessor of the order, Baisemeaux was no longer the same man. Up to that period the place which Aramis had held in the worthy governor's estimation was that of a prelate whom he respected, and a friend to whom he owed a debt of gratitude; but now he felt himself an inferior, and that Aramis was his master. He himself lighted a lantern, summoned a turnkey, and said, returning to Aramis, "I am at your orders, monseigneur." Aramis merely nodded his head, as much as to say "Very good"; and signed to him with his hand to lead the way. In this wise they reached the basement of the Bertaudière, the two first storeys of which were mounted silently and somewhat slowly; for Baisemeaux, though far from disobeying, was far from exhibiting any eagerness to obey. On arriving at the door, Baisemeaux showed a disposition to enter the prisoner's chamber; but Aramis stopping him on the threshold said, "The rules do not allow the governor to hear the prisoner's confession."

Baisemeaux bowed, and made way for Aramis, who took the lantern, and entered; and then signed to them to close the door behind him. For an instant he remained standing, listening whether Baisemeaux and the turnkey had retired; but as soon as he was assured by the sound of their dying footsteps that they had left the tower, he put the lantern on the table and gazed around. On a bed of green serge, similar in all respects to the other beds in the Bastille, save that it was newer, and under curtains half-drawn, reposed a young man. According to custom, the prisoner was without a light. At the hour of curfew, he was bound to extinguish his lamp, and we perceive how much he was favoured in being allowed to keep it burning even till then. Near the bed a large leathern armchair, with twisted legs, sustained his clothes. A little table—without pens, books, paper or ink—stood neglected in sadness near the window; while several plates, still unemptied, showed that the prisoner had scarcely touched his recent repast. Aramis saw that the young man was stretched upon his bed, his face half-concealed by his arms. The arrival of a visitor did not cause any change of position; either he was waiting in expectation, or was asleep. Aramis lighted the candle from the lantern, pushed back the armchair, and approached the bed with an evident mixture of interest and respect. The young man raised his head. "What is it?" said he.

"Have you not desired a confessor?" replied Aramis.

"Yes."

"Because you are ill?"

"Yes."

The young man gave Aramis a piercing glance. After a moment's silence, "I have seen you before," he continued. Aramis bowed.

Doubtless, the scrutiny the prisoner had just made of the cold, crafty, and imperious character stamped upon the features of the Bishop of Vannes, was little reassuring to one in his situation, for he added, "I am better."

"And then?" said Aramis.

"Why, then—being better I have no longer the same need of a confessor, I think."

"Not even of the haircloth, which the note you found in your bread informed you of?"

The young man started; but before he had either assented or denied, Aramis continued, "Not even of the ecclesiastic from whom you were to hear an important revelation?"

"If it be so," said the young man, sinking again on his pillow; "it is different. I listen."

Aramis then looked at him more closely, and was struck with the easy majesty of his mien, one which can never be acquired unless Heaven has implanted it in the blood or heart. "Sit down, monsieur," said the prisoner.

Aramis bowed and obeyed. "How does the Bastille agree with you?" asked the Bishop.

"Very well."

"You have nothing to regret?"

"Nothing."

"Not even your liberty?"

"What do you call liberty, monsieur?" asked the the prisoner with the tone of a man who is preparing for a struggle.

"I call liberty, the flowers, the air, light, the stars, the happiness of going whithersoever the nervous limbs of twenty years of age may wish to carry you."

The young man smiled, whether in resignation or contempt it was difficult to tell. "Look," said he, "I have in that Japanese vase two roses gathered yesterday evening in the bud from the governor's garden; this morning they have blown and spread their vermilion chalice beneath my gaze; with every opening petal they unfold the treasures of their perfume, filling my chamber with a fragrance that embalms it. Look now, on these two roses; even among roses these are beautiful, and the rose is the most beautiful of flowers. Why then, do you bid me desire other flowers when I possess the loveliest of all?"

Aramis gazed at the young man in surprise. "If *flowers* constitute liberty," sadly resumed the captive, "I am free, for I possess them."

"But the air," cried Aramis; "air so necessary to life!"

"Well, monsieur," returned the prisoner; "draw near to the window; it is open. Between heaven and earth the wind whirls on its storms of hail and lightning, wafts its warm mists or breathes in gentle breezes. It caresses my face.

When mounted on the back of this armchair, with my arm around the bars of the window to sustain myself, I fancy I am swimming in the wide expanse before me." The countenance of Aramis darkened as the young man continued: "Light I have! What is better than light? I have the sun, a friend who comes to visit me every day without the permission of the governor or the jailer's company. He comes in at the window and traces in my room a square the shape of the window, and which lights up the hangings of my bed down to the border. This luminous square increases from ten o'clock to midday and decreases from one till three slowly, as if, having hastened to come, it sorrowed at leaving me. When its last ray disappears I have enjoyed its presence for five hours. Is not that sufficient? I have been told that there are unhappy beings who dig in quarries, and labourers who toil in mines, and who never behold it at all." Aramis wiped the drops from his brow. "As to the stars which are so delightful to view," continued the young man, "they all resemble each other save in size and brilliancy. I am a favoured mortal, for if you had not lighted that candle you would have been able to see the beautiful stars which I was gazing at from my couch before your arrival, and whose rays were playing over my eyes." Aramis lowered his head; he felt himself overwhelmed with the bitter flow of that sinister philosophy which is the religion of the captive. "So much, then, for the flowers, the air, the daylight, and the stars," tranquilly continued the young man; "there remains but my exercise. Do I not walk all day in the governor's garden, if it is fine; here if it rains; in the fresh air if it is warm; in the warm, thanks to my winter stove, if it be cold? Ah! monsieur, do you fancy," continued the prisoner, not without bitterness, "that men have not done everything for me that a man can hope for or desire?"

"Men!" said Aramis. "Be it so; but it seems to me you forget Heaven."

"Indeed I have forgotten Heaven," answered the prisoner, with emotion; "but why do you mention it? Of what use is it to talk to a prisoner of Heaven?"

Aramis looked steadily at this singular youth who possessed the resignation of a martyr with the smile of an atheist. "Is not Heaven in everything?" he murmured in a reproachful tone.

"Say rather at the end of everything," answered the prisoner firmly.

"Be it so," said Aramis; "but let us return to our starting point."

"I desire nothing better," returned the young man.

"I am your confessor."

"Yes."

"Well, then, you ought, as a penitent, to tell me the truth."

"All that I wish is to tell it you."

"Every prisoner has committed some crime for which he has been imprisoned. What crime then have *you* committed?"

"You asked me the same question the first time you saw me," returned the prisoner.

"And then, as now, you evaded giving me an answer."

"And what reason have you for thinking that I shall now reply to you?"

"Because this time I am your confessor."

"Then if you wish me to tell what crime I have committed, explain to me in what a crime consists. For as my conscience does not accuse me, I aver that I am not a criminal."

"We are often criminals in the sight of the great of the earth, not alone for having ourselves committed crimes, but because we know that crimes have been committed."

The prisoner manifested the deepest attention. "Yes, I understand you," he said, after a pause; "yes, you are right, monsieur; it is very possible that in that light I am a criminal in the eyes of the great of the earth."

"Ah, then you know something," said Aramis, who

thought he had pierced not merely through a defect in, but through the joints of the harness.

"No, I am not aware of anything," replied the young man; "but sometimes I think—and I say to myself—"

"What do you say to yourself?"

"That if I were to think any further I should either go mad, or I should divine a great deal."

"And then—and then?" said Aramis impatiently.

"Then I leave off."

"You leave off."

"Yes; my head becomes confused and my ideas melancholy; I feel *ennui* overtaking me; I wish—"

"What?"

"I don't know; but I do not like to give myself up to longing for things which I do not possess, when I am so happy with what I have."

"You are afraid of death?" said Aramis, with a slight uneasiness.

"Yes," said the young man, smiling.

Aramis felt the chill of that smile, and shuddered.

"Oh, as you fear death you know more about matters than you say," he cried.

"And you," returned the prisoner, "who bade me to ask to see you; you, who, when I did ask for you, came here promising a world of confidence; how is it that, nevertheless, it is you who are silent, and 'tis I who speak? Since, then, we both wear masks, either let us both retain them or put them aside together."

Aramis felt the force and justice of the remark, saying to himself, "This is no ordinary man; I must be cautious. Are you ambitious?" said he suddenly to the prisoner, aloud, without preparing him for the alteration.

"What do you mean by ambition?" replied the youth.

"It is," replied Aramis, "a feeling which prompts a man to desire more than he has."

"I said that I was contented, monsieur; but, perhaps, I

deceive myself. I am ignorant of the nature of ambition; but it is not impossible I may have some. Tell me your mind; 'tis all I wish."

"An ambitious man," said Aramis, "is one who covets what is beyond his station."

"I covet nothing beyond my station," said the young man, with an assurance of manner which for the second time made the Bishop of Vannes tremble.

He was silent, but to look at the kindling eye, the knitted brow, and the reflective attitude of the captive, it was evident that he expected something more than silence—a silence which Aramis now broke. "You lied the first time I saw you," said he.

"Lied!" cried the young man, starting up on his couch, with such a tone in his voice, and such a lightning in his eyes, that Aramis recoiled, in spite of himself.

"I *should* say," returned Aramis, bowing, "you concealed from me what you knew of your infancy."

"A man's secrets are his own, monsieur," retorted the prisoner, "and not at the mercy of the first chance-comer."

"True," said Aramis, bowing still lower than before, "tis true; pardon me, but today, do I still occupy the place of a chance-comer? I beseech you to reply, monseigneur."

This title slightly disturbed the prisoner; but nevertheless he did not appear astonished that it was given him. "I do not know you, monsieur," said he.

"Oh, if I but dared, I would take your hand and would kiss it."

The young man seemed as if he were going to give Aramis his hand; but the light which beamed in his eyes faded away, and he coldly and distrustfully withdrew his hand again. "Kiss the hand of a prisoner?" he said, shaking his head. "To what purpose?"

"Why did you tell me," said Aramis, "that you were happy here? Why, that you aspired to nothing? Why, in a word, by thus speaking, do you prevent me from being frank in my turn?"

The same light shone a third time in the young man's eyes, but died ineffectually away as before.

"You distrust me?" said Aramis.

"And why say you so, monsieur?"

"Oh, for a very simple reason; if you know what you ought to know, you ought to mistrust everybody."

"Then be not astonished that I am mistrustful, since you suspect me of knowing what I know not."

Aramis was struck with admiration at this energetic resistance. "Oh, monseigneur, you drive me to despair," said he, striking the armchair with his fist.

"And, on my part, I do not comprehend you, monsieur."

"Well, then, try to understand me." The prisoner looked fixedly at Aramis.

"Sometimes it seems to me," said the latter, "that I have before me the man whom I seek, and then—"

"And then your man disappears,—is it not so?" said the prisoner, smiling. "So much the better."

Aramis rose. "Certainly," said he; "I have nothing further to say to a man who mistrusts me as you do."

"And I, monsieur," said the prisoner, in the same tone, "have nothing to say to a man who will not understand that a prisoner ought to be mistrustful of everybody."

"Even of his old friends?" said Aramis. "Oh, monseigneur, you are *too* prudent!"

"Of my old friends? You one of my old friends,— you?"

"Do you no longer remember," said Aramis, "that you once saw, in the village where your early years were spent —"

"Do you know the name of the village?" asked the prisoner.

"Noisy-le-Sec, monseigneur," answered Aramis firmly.

"Go on," said tne young man, with an immovable aspect.

"Stay, monseigneur," said Aramis; "if you are positively resolved to carry on this game, let us break off."

"I promise you," replied the prisoner, "to hear you without impatience. Only it appears to me that I have a right to repeat the question I have already asked— 'Who are you?' "

"Do you remember, fifteen or eighteen years ago, seeing at Noisy-le-Sec a cavalier accompanied by a lady in black silk, with flame-coloured ribands in her hair?"

"Yes," said the young man; "I once asked the name of this cavalier, and they told me he called himself the Abbé d'Herblay. I was astonished that the Abbé had so warlike an air, and they replied that there was nothing singular in that, seeing that he was one of Louis XIII's musketeers."

"Well," said Aramis, "that musketeer and Abbé, afterwards Bishop of Vannes, is your confessor now."

"I knew it; I recognised you."

"Then, monseigneur, if you know that, I must further add a fact of which you are ignorant—that if the King were to know this evening of the presence of this musketeer, this Abbé, this bishop, this confessor, *here*—he, who has risked everything to visit you, would tomorrow see glitter the executioner's axe at the bottom of a dungeon more gloomy and more obscure than yours."

While hearing these words, delivered with emphasis, the young man had raised himself on his couch, and gazed more and more eagerly at Aramis.

The result of his scrutiny was that he appeared to derive some confidence from it. "Yes," he murmured, "I remember perfectly. The woman of whom you speak came once with you, and twice afterwards with another." He hesitated.

"With another woman, who came to see you every month,—is it not so, monseigneur?"

"Yes."

"Do you know who this lady was?"

The light seemed ready to flash from the prisoner's eyes. "I am aware that she was one of the ladies of the court," he said.

"You remember that lady well, do you not?"

"Oh, my recollection can hardly be very confused on this head," said the young prisoner. "I saw that lady once with a gentleman about forty-five years old. I saw her once with you, and with the lady dressed in black. I have seen her twice since with the same person. These four people, with my master, and old Perronnette, my jailer, and the governor of the prison, are the only persons with whom I have ever spoken, and indeed, almost the only persons I have ever seen."

"Then you were in prison?"

"If I am a prisoner here, there I was comparatively free, although in a very narrow sense—a house which I never quitted, a garden surrounded with walls I could not clear, these constituted my residence; but you know it, as you have been there. In a word, being accustomed to live within these bounds, I never cared to leave them. And so you will understand, monsieur, that not having seen anything of the world, I have nothing left to care for; and therefore, if you relate anything, you will be obliged to explain everything to me."

"And I will do so," said Aramis bowing, "for it is my duty, monseigneur."

"Well, then, begin by telling me who was my tutor."

"A worthy and, above all, an honourable gentleman, monseigneur; fit guide both for body and soul. Had you ever any reason to complain of him?"

"Oh, no; quite the contrary. But this gentleman of yours often used to tell me that my father and mother were dead. Did he deceive me, or did he speak the truth?"

"He was compelled to comply with the orders given him."

"Then he lied?"

"In one respect. Your father is dead."

"And my mother?"

"She is dead for you."

"But then she lives for others, does she not?"

"Yes."

"And I—and I, then," 'the young man looked sharply at Aramis',"am compelled to live in the obscurity of a prison?"

"Alas ! I fear so."

"And that, because my presence in the world would lead to the revelation of a great secret?"

"Certainly a very great secret."

"My enemy must indeed be powerful, to be able to shut up in the Bastille a child such as I then was."

"He is. Listen, then; I will in a few words tell you what has passed in France during the last twenty-three or twenty-four years; that is, from the probable date of your birth; in a word, from the time that interests you."

"Say on." And the young man resumed his serious and attentive attitude.

"Do you know who was the son of Henry IV?"

"At least I know who his successor was."

"How?"

"By means of a coin dated 1610, which bears the effigy of Henry IV; and another of 1612, bearing that of Louis XIII. So I presumed that, there being only two years between the two dates, Louis was Henry's successor."

"Then," said Aramis, "you know that the last reigning monarch was Louis XIII?"

"I do," answered the youth, slightly reddening.

"Well, he was a prince full of noble ideas and great projects, always, alas! deferred by the troubles of the times and the struggles that his minister Richelieu had to maintain against the great nobles of France. The King himself was of a feeble character; and died young and unhappy."

"I know it."

"He had been long anxious about having an heir; a care which weighs heavily on princes, who desire to leave behind them more than one pledge that their thoughts and works will be continued."

"Did the King, then, die childless?" asked the prisoner, smiling.

"No, but he was long without one, and for a long while thought he should be the last of his race. This idea had reduced him to the depths of despair, when suddenly, his wife, Anne of Austria—"

The prisoner trembled.

"Did you know," said Aramis, "that Louis XIII's wife was called Anne of Austria?"

"Continue," said the young man, without replying to the question.

"When suddenly," resumed Aramis, "the Queen announced an interesting event. There was great joy at the intelligence, and all prayed for her happy delivery. On the 5th of September, 1638, she gave birth to a son"

Here Aramis looked at his companion, and thought he observed him turning pale. "You are about to hear," said Aramis, "an account which few could now give; for it refers to a secret which they think buried with the dead or entombed in the abyss of the confessional."

"And you will tell me this secret?" broke in the youth.

"Oh!" said Aramis with unmistakable emphasis, "I do not know that I ought to risk this secret by entrusting it to one who has no desire to quit the Bastille."

"I hear you, monsieur."

"The Queen, then, gave birth to a son. But while the court was rejoicing over the event, when the King had shown the new-born child to the nobility and people and was sitting gaily down to table to celebrate the event, the Queen, who was alone in her room, was again taken ill, and gave birth to a second son."

"Oh!" said the prisoner, betraying a better acquaintance with the affair than he had owned to, "I thought that Monsieur was only born a—"

Aramis raised his finger: "Let me continue," he said.

The prisoner sighed impatiently, and paused.

"Yes," said Aramis, "the Queen had a second son, whom dame Perronnette, the midwife, received in her arms."

"Dame Perronnette!" murmured the young man.

"They ran at once to the banqueting-room, and whispered to the King what had happened; he rose and quitted the table. But this time it was no longer happiness that his face expressed, but something akin to terror. The birth of twins changed into bitterness the joy to which that of an only son had given rise, seeing that in France (a fact you are assuredly ignorant of) it is the oldest of the King's sons who succeeds his father."

"I know it."

"And that the doctors and jurists assert that there is ground for doubting whether he who first makes his appearance is the elder by the law of Heaven and of nature."

The prisoner uttered a smothered cry, and became whiter than the coverlet under which he hid himself.

"Well," continued Aramis; "this is what they relate, what they declare; this is why one of the Queen's two sons, shamefully parted from his brother, shamefully sequestered, is buried in the profoundest obscurity; this is why that second son has disappeared, and so completely, that not a soul in France, save his mother, is aware of his existence."

"Yes, his mother who has cast him off!" cried the prisoner in a tone of despair.

"Except, also," Aramis went on, "the lady in the black dress; and finally, excepting—"

"Excepting yourself—is it not? You, who come and relate all this; you, who arouse in my soul curiosity, hatred, ambition, and, perhaps, even the thirst of vengeance; except you, monsieur, who, if you are the man whom I expect, whom the note I have received applies to; whom, in short, Heaven ought to send me, must possess about you—"

"What?" asked Aramis.

"A portrait of the King, Louis XIV, who at this moment reigns upon the throne of France."

"Here is the portrait," replied the Bishop, handing the prisoner a miniature in enamel, on which Louis was depicted, life-like, with a handsome, lofty mien. The prisoner eagerly seized the portrait, and gazed at it with devouring eyes.

"And now, monseigneur," said Aramis, "here is a mirror." Aramis left the prisoner time to recover his ideas.

"So high!—so high!" murmured the young man, eagerly comparing the likeness of Louis with his own countenance reflected in the glass.

"What do you think of it?" at length said Aramis.

"I think that I am lost," replied the captive; "the King will never set me free."

"And I—I demand," added the Bishop, fixing his piercing eyes significantly upon the prisoner, "I demand which of the two is the King; the one whom this miniature portrays, or whom the glass reflects?"

"The King, monsieur," sadly replied the young man, "is he who is on the throne, who is not in prison; and who, on the other hand, can cause others to be entombed here. Royalty is power; and you see well how powerless I am."

"Monseigneur," answered Aramis, with a respect he had not yet manifested, "the King, mark me, will, if you desire it, be he who, quitting his dungeon, shall maintain himself upon the throne, on which his friends will place him."

"By which you mean—"

"That if I restore you your place on your brother's throne, he shall take yours in prison."

"Alas, there is so much suffering in prison, especially to a man who has drunk so deeply of the cup of enjoyment."

"Your Royal Highness will always be free to act as you may desire; and if it seems good to you, after punishment, may pardon."

"Good. And now, are you aware of one thing, monsieur?"

"Tell me, my Prince."

"It is that I will hear nothing further from you till I am clear of the Bastille."

"I was going to say to your Highness that I should only have the pleasure of seeing you once again."

"And when?"

"The day when my Prince leaves these gloomy walls."

"Heavens! How will you give me notice of it?"

"By myself coming to fetch you."

"Yourself?"

"My Prince, do not leave this chamber save with me, or if in my absence you are compelled to do so, remember that I am not concerned in it."

"And so I am not to speak a word of this to anyone whatever, save to you."

"Save only to me." Aramis bowed very low.

The Prince offered his hand to Aramis, who sank upon his knee and kissed it.

"It is the first act of homage paid to our future King," said he. "When I see you again, I shall say, 'Good-day, sire.'"

"Till then," said the young man, pressing his wan and wasted fingers over his heart,—'till then, no more dreams, no more strain upon my life—it would break! Oh, monsieur, how small is my prison—how low the window—how narrow are the doors! To think that so much pride, splendour, and happiness should be able to enter in and remain here!"

"Your Royal Highness makes me proud," said Aramis, "since you infer it is I who brought all this." And he rapped immediately on the door. The jailer came to open it with Baisemeaux, who, devoured by fear and uneasiness, was beginning, in spite of himself, to listen at the door. Happily, neither of the speakers had forgotten to smother his voice, even in the most passionate outbreaks.

"What a confessor!" said the governor, forcing a laugh. "Who would believe that a mere recluse, a man almost dead, could have committed crimes so numerous, and so long to tell of?"

Aramis made no reply. He was eager to leave the Bastille, where the secret which overwhelmed him seemed to double the weight of the walls. As soon as they reached Baisemeaux's quarters, "Let us proceed to business, my dear governor," said Aramis.

"Alas!" replied Baisemeaux.

"You have to ask me for my receipt for one hundred and fifty thousand livres," said the Bishop.

"And to pay over the first third of the sum," added the poor governor, with a sigh, taking three steps towards his iron strong-box.

"Here is the receipt," said Aramis.

"And here is the money," returned Baisemeaux, with a threefold sigh.

"The order instructed me only to give a receipt; it said nothing about receiving the money," rejoined Aramis. "Adieu, Monsieur le Gouverneur!"

And he departed, leaving Baisemeaux almost more than stifled with joy and surprise at this regal present, so liberally bestowed by the confessor extraordinary to the Bastille.

5

Another Supper At The Bastille

Seven o'clock sounded from the great clock of the Bastille, that famous clock, which like all the accessories of the state prison, the very use of which is a torture, recalled to the prisoners' minds the destination of every hour of their punishment. This same hour was that of M. le Gouverneur's supper also. He had a guest today, and the spit turned more heavily than usual. Baisemeaux, seated at table, was rubbing his hands and looking at the Bishop of Vannes, who, booted like a cavalier, dressed in grey, and sword at side, kept talking of his hunger and testifying the liveliest impatience. M. de Baisemeaux de Montlezun was not accustomed to the unbending movements of his greatness, my Lord of Vannes, and this evening Aramis, becoming quite sprightly, volunteered confidence on confidence. The prelate had again a little touch of the musketeer about him. The Bishop just trenched on the borders only of licence in his style of conversation. As for M. de Baisemeaux, with the facility of vulgar people, he gave himself up entirely upon this point of his guest's freedom. "Monsieur," said he, "for indeed tonight I dare not call you monseigneur."

"By no means," said Aramis; "call me monsieur, I am booted."

"Do you know, monsieur, of whom you remind me this evening?"

"No, faith," said Aramis, taking up his glass; "but I hope I remind you of a capital guest."

"You remind me of two, monsieur. François, shut the window; the wind may annoy his greatness."

"And let him go," added Aramis. "The supper is completely served, and we shall eat it very well without waiters. I like extremely to be tête-à-tête when I am with a friend." Baisemeaux bowed respectfully. "I like extremely," continued Aramis, "to help myself."

"Retire, François," cried Baisemeaux. "I was saying that your greatness puts me in mind of two persons; one, very illustrious, the late Cardinal, the great Cardinal de la Rochelle, who wore boots like you."

"Indeed," said Aramis; "and the other?"

"The other was a certain musketeer, very handsome, very brave, very adventurous, very fortunate, who, from being abbé, turned musketeer, and from musketeer turned abbé." Aramis condescended to smile. "From abbé," continued Baisemeaux, encouraged by Aramis's smile—"from abbé, bishop and from bishop—"

"Ah, stay there, I beg," exclaimed Aramis.

"I say, monsieur, that you gave me the idea of a cardinal."

"Enough, dear M. Baisemeaux. As you said, I have on the boots of a cavalier, but I do not intend, for all that, to embroil myself with the church this evening."

"But you have wicked intentions, however, monseigneur."

"Oh, yes, wicked I own, as everything mundane is."

"You traverse the town and the streets in disguise?"

"In disguise, as you say."

"And do you still make use of your sword?"

"Yes, I should think so; but only when I am compelled."

"Do you not think," said M. de Baisemeaux, "that you will find yourself very lonely now M. de la Fère has returned to his household gods at Blois? He is a very old friend, is he not?"

"You know it as I do, Baisemeaux, seeing that you were in the musketeers with us."

"Bah! With my friends I reckon neither bottles of wine nor years."

"And you do right; but I do more than love M. de la Fère, dear Baisemeaux—, I venerate him."

"Well, for my part, though 'tis singular," said the governor, "I prefer M. d'Artagnan to him. There is a man for you, who drinks long and well! That kind of people allow you at least to penetrate their thoughts."

"Baisemeaux, make me tipsy tonight; let us have a debauch as of old, and if I have a trouble at the bottom of my heart, I promise you, you shall see it as you would a diamond at the bottom of your glass."

"Bravo!" said Baisemeaux, and he poured out a great glass of wine and drank it off at a draught, trembling with joy at the idea of being, by hook or by crook, in the secret of some high archi-episcopal misdemeanour. While he was drinking he did not see with what attention Aramis was noting the sounds in the great court. A courier came in about eight o'clock as François brought in the fifth bottle, and, although the courier made a great noise, Baisemeaux heard nothing.

"The devil take him," said Aramis.

"What ? Who?" asked Baisemeaux. "I hope 'tis neither the wine you drink nor he who is the cause of your drinking it."

"No; it is a horse, who is making noise enough in the court for a whole squadron."

"Pooh! Some courier or other," replied the governor, redoubling his numerous bumpers. "Yes; and may the devil take him, and so quickly that we shall never hear him speak more! Hurrah! Hurrah!"

"You forget me, Baisemeaux! My glass is empty," said Aramis, showing his dazzling goblet.

François re-entered; Baisemeaux took from his hands the minister's order. He slowly undid it, and as slowly read it. Aramis pretended to be drinking, so as to be able to watch his host through the glass.

Then, Baisemeaux having read it: "What was I just saying?" he exclaimed.

"What is it?" asked the Bishop.

"An order of release! There, now; excellent news indeed to disturb us!"

"Excellent news for him whom it concerns, you will at least agree, my dear governor!"

"And at eight o'clock in the evening!"

"It is charitable!"

"Oh, charity is all very well, but it is for that fellow who says he is so weary and tired, but not for me who am amusing myself," said Baisemeaux, exasperated.

"Will you lose by him, then? And is the prisoner who is to be set at liberty a high payer?"

"Oh, yes, indeed—a miserable, five-franc rat!"

"Let me see it," asked M. d'Herblay. "It is no indiscretion?"

"By no means; read it."

"There is 'Urgent', on the paper; you have seen that, I suppose?"

"And so I shall strictly obey; and tomorrow morning at daybreak, the prisoner referred to shall be set free."

"Tomorrow?"

"At dawn."

"Why not this evening, seeing that the *lettre de cachet* bears, both on the direction and inside, '*urgent* '."

"Because this evening we are at supper, and our affairs are urgent too!"

"Dear Baisemeaux, booted though I be, I feel myself a priest, and charity has higher claims upon me than hunger and thirst. This unfortunate man has suffered long enough, since you have just told me that he has been your prisoner these ten years. Abridge his suffering. His good time has come; give him the benefit quickly. God will repay you in Paradise with years of felicity."

"You wish it?"

"I entreat you."

"What! In the very middle of our repast"

"I implore you; such an action is worth ten Benedicites."

"It shall be as you desire, only our supper will get cold."

"Oh, never heed that."

Baisemeaux leaned back to ring for François, and by a very natural motion turned round towards the door. The order had remained on the table; Aramis seized the opportunity when Baisemeaux was not looking to change the paper for another, folded in the same manner, and which he took from his pocket. "François," said the governor, "let the major come up here with the turnkeys of the Bertaudière." François bowed and quitted the room, leaving the two companions alone.

6

The General Of The Order

There was now a brief silence, during which Aramis never removed his eyes from Baisemeaux for a moment. The latter seemed only half decided to disturb himself thus in the middle of supper, and it was clear he was seeking some pretext, whether good or bad, for delay, at any rate till after dessert. And it appeared also that he had hit upon a pretext at last.

"Eh, but it is impossible," he cried.

"How impossible?" said Aramis. "Give me a glimpse of this impossibility."

"'Tis impossible to set a prisoner at liberty at such an hour. Where can he go to, he, who is unacquainted with Paris?"

"He will go wherever he can."

"You see, now, one might as well set a blind man free!"

"I have a carriage, and will take him wherever he wishes.

"You have an answer for everything. François, tell the major to go and open the cell of M. Seldon, No. 3, Bertaudière."

"Seldon!" exclaimed Aramis, very naturally. "You said Seldon, I think?"

"I said Seldon, of course. 'Tis the name of the man they set free."

"Oh, you meant to say Marchiali?" said Aramis.

"Marchiali? Oh, yes, indeed. No, no, Seldon."

"I think you are making a mistake, Monsieur Baisemeaux."

"I have read the order."

"And I also."

"And I saw 'Seldon' in letters as large as that," and Baisemeaux held up his finger.

"And I read 'Marchiali' in characters as large as this," said Aramis, also holding up two fingers.

"To the proof; let us throw a light on the matter," said Baisemeaux, confident he was right. "There is the paper, you have only to read it."

"I read 'Marchiali', " returned Aramis, spreading out the paper. "Look."

Baisemeaux looked, and his arms dropped suddenly.

"Yes, yes," he said, quite overwhelmed; "yes, Marchiali. 'Tis plainly written Marchiali! Quite true!"

"Ah!"

"How? The man of whom we have talked so much? The man whom they are every day telling me to take such care of?"

"There is 'Marchiali', " repeated the inflexible Aramis.

"I must own it, monseigneur. But I understand absolutely nothing about it."

"You believe your eyes, at any rate."

"To tell me very plainly there is 'Marchiali'. "

"And in a good handwriting, too."

"'Tis a wonder! I still see this order and the name of Seldon, Irishman. I see it. Ah! I even recollect that under this name there was a blot of ink."

"No, there is no ink; no, there is no blot."

"Oh, but there was, though; I know it, because I rubbed the powder that was over the blot."

"In a word, be it how it may, dear M. Baisemeaux," said Aramis, "and whatever you may have seen, the order is signed to release Marchiali, blot or no blot."

"The order is signed to release Marchiali," repeated Baisemeaux mechanically, endeavouring to regain his courage.

"And you are going to release this prisoner. If your heart dictates to you to deliver Seldon also, I declare to you I will

not oppose it the least in the world." Aramis accompanied
the remark with a smile, the irony of which effectually dis-
pelled Baisemeaux's confusion of mind, and restored his
courage.

"Monseigneur," he said, "this Marchiali is the very same
prisoner whom the other day a priest, confessor of *our order*, came to visit in so imperious and so secret a manner."

"I don't know that, monsieur," replied the Bishop.

"'Tis no such long time ago, dear Monsieur d'Herblay."

"It is true. But *with us*, monsieur, it is good that the man
of today should no longer know what the man of yesterday
did."

"In any case," said Baisemeaux, "the visit of this Jesuit
confessor must have given happiness to this man."

Aramis made no reply, but recommended eating and drinking. As for Baisemeaux, no longer touching anything that
was on the table, he again took up the order and examined
it in every way. This investigation, under ordinary circumstances, would have made the ears of the impatient Aramis
burn with anger; but the Bishop of Vannes did not become
incensed for so little, above all, when he had murmured to
himself that to do so was dangerous. "Are you going to
release Marchiali?" he said. "What mellow and fragrant
sherry this is, my dear governor."

"Monseigneur," replied Baisemeaux, "I shall release the
prisoner Marchiali when I have summoned the courier who
brought the order, and above all, when, by interrogating
him, I have satisfied myself."

"The order is sealed, and the courier is ignorant of the
contents. What do you want to satisfy yourself about?"

"Be it so, monseigneur; but I shall send to the ministry,
and M. de Lyonne will either confirm or withdraw the order."

"What is the good of all that?" asked Aramis coldly.

"What good?"

"Yes; what is your object, I ask?"

"The object of never deceiving oneself, monseigneur, nor being wanting in the respect which a subaltern owes to his superior officers, nor infringing the duties of that service which one has voluntarily accepted."

"Very good; you have just spoken so eloquently that I cannot but admire you. It is true that a subaltern owes respect to his superiors; he is guilty when he deceives himself, and he should be punished if he infringes either the duties or laws of his office."

Baisemeaux looked at the Bishop with astonishment.

"It follows," pursued Aramis, "that you are going to ask advice, to put your conscience at ease in the matter?"

"Yes, monseigneur."

"And if a superior officer gives you orders, you will obey?"

"Never doubt it, monseigneur."

"Well, Monsieur de Baisemeaux," said Aramis, bending an eagle glance on the governor, "I adopt so frankly your doubts, and your mode of clearing them up, that I will take a pen, if you will give me one."

Baisemeaux gave him a pen.

"And a sheet of white paper," added Aramis.

Baisemeaux handed some paper.

"Now, I—I, also—I, here present—incontestably, I—am going to write an order to which I am certain you will give credence, incredulous as you are!"

Baisemeaux turned pale at this icy assurance of manner. It seemed to him that that voice of the Bishop, but just now so playful and so gay, had become funereal and sad; that the waxlights changed into the tapers of a mortuary chapel, and the glasses of wine into chalices of blood.

Aramis took a pen and wrote. Baisemeaux, in terror read over his shoulder.

"A.M.D.G." wrote the Bishop; and he drew a cross under these four letters, which signify *ad majorem Dei gloriam*, "to the greater glory of God"; and thus he continued, "It is our pleasure that the order brought to M. de Baisemeaux de Montlezun, governor, for the King, of the castle of the Bastille, be held good and effectual, and be immediately carried into operation.

"(Signed)D'HERBLAY,

"General of the Order, by the Grace of God."

Baisemeaux was so profoundly astonished, that his features remained contracted, his lips parted, and his eyes fixed.

"Come, come," said Aramis, after a long silence, during which the governor of the Bastille had slowly recovered his senses, "do not lead me to believe, dear Baisemeaux, that the presence of the General of the Order is as terrible as His, and that men die merely from having seen Him. Take courage; rouse yourself; give me your hand, and obey."

Baisemeaux, reassured, if not satisfied, obeyed, kissed Aramis's hand, and rose. "Immediately?" he murmured.

"What is the process for releasing a prisoner?"

"I have the regulations."

"Well, then, follow the regulations, my friend."

"I go with my major to the prisoner's room, and conduct him, if he is a personage of importance."

"But this Marchiali is not an important personage," said Aramis carelessly.

"I don't know," answered the governor; as if he would have said, "It is for you to instruct me."

"Then, if you don't know it, I am right; so act towards Marchiali as you act towards one of obscure station."

"Good; the regulations so provide. They are to the effect that the turnkey, or one of the lower officials, shall bring the prisoner before the governor, in the office."

"Well, 'tis very wise, that; and then?"

"Then we return to the prisoner the valuables he wore at the time of his imprisonment, his clothes and papers, if the minister's order has not otherwise directed."

"What was the minister's order as to this Marchiali?"

"Nothing; for the unhappy man arrived here without jewels, without papers, and almost without clothes."

"See how simple it all is. Indeed, Baisemeaux, you make a mountain of everything. Remain here, and make them bring the prisoner to the governor's house."

Baisemeaux obeyed. He summoned his lieutenant, and gave him an order, which the latter passed on, without disturbing himself about it, to the next whom it concerned.

Half an hour afterwards they heard a gate shut in the court; it was the door to the dungeon, which had just rendered up its prey to the free air. Aramis blew out all the candles which lighted the room but one, which he left burning behind the door. This flickering glare prevented the sight from resting steadily on any object. It multiplied tenfold the changing forms and shadows of the place, by its wavering uncertainty. Steps drew near.

"Go and meet your men," said Aramis to Baisemeaux.

The governor obeyed. The sergeant and turnkeys disappeared. Baisemeaux re-entered, followed by a prisoner. Aramis had placed himself in the shade; he saw without being seen. Baisemeaux, in an agitated tone of voice, made the young man acquainted with the order which set him at liberty. The prisoner listened without making a single gesture, or saying a word.

"You will swear ('tis the regulation that requires it)," added the governor, "never to reveal anything that you have seen or heard in the Bastille."

The prisoner perceived a crucifix; he stretched out his hands, and swore with his lips. "And now, monsieur, you are free; whither do you intend going?"

The prisoner turned his head, as if looking behind him for some protection, on which he ought to rely. Then was it that Aramis came out of the shade: "I am here," he said, "to render the gentleman whatever service he may please to ask."

The prisoner slightly reddened, and without hesitation

passed his arm through that of Aramis. "God have you in His holy keeping," he said, in a voice the firmness of which made the governor tremble as much as the form of the blessing astonished him.

Aramis, on shaking hands with Baisemeaux, said to him: "Does my order trouble you? Do you fear their finding it here, should they come to search?"

"I desire to keep it, monseigneur," said Baisemeaux. "If they found it here it would be a certain indication I should be lost, and in that case you would be a powerful and a last auxiliary for me."

"Being your accomplice, you mean?" answered Aramis, shrugging his shoulders. "*Adieu*, Baisemeaux," said he.

The horses were in waiting, making the carriage shake again with their impatience. Baisemeaux accompanied the Bishop to the bottom of the steps. Aramis caused his companion to mount before him, then followed, and without giving the driver any further order, "Go on," said he. The carriage rattled over the pavement of the courtyard. An officer with a torch went before the horses, and gave orders at every post to let them pass. During the time taken in opening all the barriers, Aramis barely breathed, and you might have heard his "sealed heart knock against his ribs." The prisoner, buried in a corner of the carriage, made no more sign of life than his companion. At length a jolt more severe than the others announced to them that they had cleared the last watercourse. Behind the carriage closed the last gate, that in the Rue St Antoine. No more walls either on the right or left; heaven everywhere, liberty everywhere, and life everywhere. The horses, kept in check by a vigorous hand, went quietly as far as the middle of the faubourg. There they began to trot. Little by little, whether they warmed over it, or whether they were urged, they gained in swiftness, and once past Bercy, the carriage seemed to fly, so great was the ardour of the course's. These horses ran thus as far as Villeneuve St Georges, where relays were waiting. Then four instead of two whirled the carriage away in the direction of Mehun, and pulled up for a moment in the middle of the forest of Sénart. No doubt the order had been given the postilion beforehand, for Aramis had no occasion even to make a sign.

"What is the matter?" asked the prisoner, as if waking from a long dream.

"The matter is, monseigneur," said Aramis, "that before going further, it is necessary your Royal Highness and I should converse."

"I will wait an opportunity, monsieur," answered the young Prince.

"We could not have a better, monseigneur; we are in the middle of a forest, and no one can hear us."

"The postilion?"

"The postilion of this relay is deaf and dumb, monseigneur."

"I am at your service, M. d'Herblay."

"Is it your pleasure to remain in the carriage?"

"Yes, we are comfortably seated, and I like this carriage, for it has restored me to liberty."

"Wait, monseigneur; there is yet a precaution to be taken."

"What?"

"We are here on the highway; cavaliers or carriages travelling like ourselves might pass, and seeing us stopping deem us in some difficulty. Let us avoid offers of assistance which would embarrass us."

"Give the postilion orders to conceal the carriage in one of the side avenues."

" 'Tis exactly what I wished to do, monseigneur."

Aramis made a sign to the deaf and dumb driver of the carriage, whom he touched on the arm. The latter dismounted, took the leaders by the bridle, and led them over the velvet sward and the mossy grass of a winding alley, at the bottom of which, on this moonless night, the deep shades formed a curtain blacker than ink. This done, the man lay down on a slope near his horses, who, on either side, kept nibbling the young oak shoots.

"I am listening," said the young Prince to Aramis; "but what are you doing there?"

"I am disarming myself of my pistols, of which we have no further need, monseigneur."

7

Crown And Tiara

"My prince," said Aramis, turning in the carriage towards his companion.

"I listen," said the young prince.

"Monseigneur," resumed Aramis, "you know the history of the government which today controls France. The King issued from an infancy imprisoned like yours, obscure as yours, and confined as yours; only, instead of ending, like yourself, this slavery in a prison—this obscurity in solitude—these straitened circumstances in concealment, he was fain to bear all these miseries, humiliations, and distresses, in full daylight, under the pitiless sun of royalty; or an elevation so flooded with light, where every stain appears a miserable blemish and every glory a stain. The King has suffered; it rankles in his mind; and he will avenge himself. He will be a bad king. I say not that he will pour out blood, like Louis XI or Charles IX, for he has no mortal injuries to avenge; but he will devour the means and substance of his people; for he has himself undergone wrongs in his own interest and money. In the first place, then, I quite acquit my conscience when I consider openly the merits and faults of this Prince; and if I condemn him, my conscience absolves me."

"Tell me plainly, monsieur—tell me without disguise—what I am today, and what you aim at my being tomorrow."

"You are Philippe, the son of King Louis XIII, brother of Louis XIV, natural and legitimate heir to the throne of France. In keeping you near him as Monsieur has been kept—Monsieur, your younger brother—the King reserved to himself the right of being legitimate sovereign. The doctors only could dispute his legitimacy. But the doctors always prefer the King who is, to the king who is not. Providence has willed that you should be persecuted; and this persecution today consecrates you King of France. You had then a right to reign, seeing that it is disputed; had a right to be proclaimed, seeing that you have been concealed; and you possess royal blood, since no one had dared to shed yours, as your servants, has been shed. Now see, then, what this Providence, which you have so often accused of having in every way thwarted you, has done for you. It has given you the features, figure, age, and voice of your brother; and the very causes of your persecution are about to become those of your triumphant restoration. Tomorrow, after tomorrow—from the very first, regal phantom, living shade of Louis XIV, you will sit upon his throne, whence the will of Heaven, confided in execution to the arm of man, will have hurled him, without hope of return."

"I understand," said the Prince, "my brother's blood will not be shed, then."

"You will be sole arbiter of his fate."

"The secret of which they made an evil use against me?"

"You will employ it against him. What did he do to conceal it? He concealed you. Living image of himself, you will defeat the conspiracy of Mazarin and Anne of Austria. You, my Prince, will have the same interest in concealing him who will, as a prisoner, resemble you, as you will resemble him as king."

"I fall back on what I was saying to you. Who will guard him?"

"Who guarded you?"

"You know this secret—you have made use of it with regard to myself. Who else knows it?"

"The Queen-Mother."

"What will she do?"

"Nothing, if you choose."

"How is that?"

"How can she recognise you, if you act in a manner that no one can recognise you?"

"Tis true; but there are grave difficulties."

"State them, Prince."

"My brother is married; I cannot take my brother's wife."

"I will cause Spain to consent to a divorce; it is in the interest of your new policy; it is human morality. All that is really noble and really useful in this world will find its account therein."

"The imprisoned King will speak."

"To whom do you think he should speak—to the walls?" You mean by walls, the men in whom you put confidence."

"If need be, yes. And besides, Your Royal Highness—"

"I will exile the deposed King," interrupted Philippe, shuddering; "it will be more humane."

"The King's good pleasure will decide the point," said Aramis. "But has the problem been well put? Have I brought out the solution according to the wishes or the foresight of your Royal Highness?"

"Yes, monsieur, yes; you have forgotten nothing," and Philippe, seizing his hand in a quick, agitated manner, exclaimed,—

"Let us go where the crown of France is to be found !"

"Is this your decision, monseigneur?" asked Aramis.

"It is."

"Irrevocably so?"

Philippe did not even deign to reply. He gazed earnestly at the Bishop, as if to ask him if it were possible for a man to waver after having once made up his mind.

"These looks are flashes of fire, which portray character," said Aramis, bowing over Philippe's hand. "You will be great, monseigneur; I will answer for that."

The carriage sped them rapidly along the road leading to Vaux-1e-Vicomte.

8

The Château De Vaux-Le-Vicomte

The Château of Vaux-1e-Vicomte, situated about a league from Mélun, had been built by Fouquet, Superintendent of Finances, in 1655, at a time when there was a scarcity of money in France; Mazarin as Cardinal had taken all that there was, and Fouquet expended the remainder.

This magnificent palace had now been got ready for the reception of the greatest reigning sovereign of the time. M. Fouquet's friends had transported thither, some their actors and their dresses, others their troops of sculptors and artists; not forgetting others with their ready-mended pens. The cascades, somewhat rebellious nymphs though they were, poured forth their waters brighter and clearer than crystal; they scattered over the bronze tritons and nereids their waves of foam which glistened like fire in the rays of the sun. An army of servants were hurrying to and fro in squadrons in the courtyard and corridors; while Fouquet, who had only that morning arrived, walked all through the palace with a calm, observant glance, in order to give his last orders, after his intendants had inspected everything.

It was the 15th of August. The sun poured down its burning rays upon the heathen deities of marble and bronze; it raised the temperature of the water in the conch shells, and ripened on the walls those magnificent peaches.

With a perfect reliance that arrangements had been made fairly to distribute the vast number of guests throughout the palace, and that he had not omitted to attend to any of the internal regulations for their comfort, Fouquet devoted his entire attention to the *ensemble* alone. He saw Aramis on the staircase. The prelate beckoned to him. The Superintendant joined his friend.

"In an hour—" said Aramis.

"In an hour!" replied Fouquet, sighing.

"And the people who ask one another what is the good of these royal fêtes!" continued the Bishop of Vannes, laughing, with his false smile.

"Alas! I, too, who am not the people, ask the same thing."

"I will answer you in four-and-twenty hours, monseigneur. Assume a cheerful countenance, for it should be a day of true rejoicing."

"Well, believe me or not, as you like, d'Herblay," said the Superintendant, with a swelling heart, pointing at the *cortège* of Louis, visible in the horizon, "he certainly loves me but very little, nor do I care much for him; but I cannot tell you how it is, that since he is approaching towards my house—"

"Well, what?"

"Well, then, since I know he is on his way here, as my guest, he is more sacred than ever for me; he is my acknowledged sovereign, and as such is very dear to me. Though I know he does not trust one, I feel that if he were really to wish it, I could love that young man."

"You should not say that to me," returned Aramis, "but rather to M. Colbert, the Intendant."

"To M. Colbert!" exclaimed Fouquet. "Why so?"

"Because he would allow you a pension out of the King's privy purse, as soon as he becomes Superintendant. He covets that position, you know," said Aramis, preparing to leave as soon as he had dealt this last blow.

"Where are you going?" returned Fouquet, with gloomy look.

"To my own apartment, in order to change my costume, monseigneur."

"Whereabouts are you lodging, d'Herblay?"

"In the blue room on the second storey."

"The room immediately over the King"s room?"

"Precisely."

"You will be subject to very great restraint there. What an idea to condemn yourself to a room where you cannot stir or move about."

"During the night, monseigneur, I sleep or read in my bed."

"And your servants?"

"I have only one person with me. I find my reader quite sufficient. *Adieu*, monseigneur; do not over-fatigue yourself keep yourself fresh for the arrival of the King."

9

Nectar And Ambrosia

M. Fouquet held the stirrup of the King, who, having dismounted, bowed most graciously, and more graciously still held out his hand to him, which Fouquet, in spite of a slight resistance on the King's part, carried respectfully to his lips. The King wished to wait in the first courtyard for the arrival of the carriages, nor had he long to wait, for the roads had been put into excellent order by the Superintendant, and a stone would hardly have been found of the size of an egg the whole way from Mélun to Vaux; so that the carriages, rolling along as though on a carpet, brought the ladies to Vaux, without jolting or fatigue, by eight o'clock. They were received by Madame Fouquet, and at the moment they made their appearance, a light as bright as day burst forth from all the trees and vases and marble statues. This species of enchantment lasted until their Majesties had retired into the palace. All these wonders and magical effects which the chronicler has heaped up, or rather preserved, in his recital, at the risk of rivalling the creations of a romancist; these splendours, whereby night seemed conquered and nature corrected, together with every delight and luxury combined for the satisfaction of all the senses, as well as of the mind, Fouquet did in real truth offer to his sovereign in that enchanting retreat of which no monarch could at that time boast of possessing an equal. We do not intend to describe the grand banquet, at which all the royal guests were present, nor the concerts, nor the fairy-like and magical transformations and metamorphoses; it will be more than enough for our purpose to depict the countenance which the King assumed.

As soon as his hunger was appeased, the King became dull and gloomy; the more so in proportion to the satisfaction he fancied he had manifested, and particularly on account of the deferential manner which his courtiers had shown towards Fouquet. D'Artagnan, who ate a good deal and drank but little, without allowing it to be noticed, did not lose a single opportunity, but made a great number of observations which he turned to good profit.

When the supper was finished, the King expressed a wish not to lose the promenade. The park was illuminated; the moon, too, as if she had placed herself at the orders of the lord of Vaux, silvered the trees and lakes with her bright phosphoric light. The air was soft and balmy; the gravelled walks through the thickly set avenues yielded luxuriously to the feet. The fête was complete in every respect, for the King, having met La Vallière in one of the winding paths of the wood, was able to press her by the hand and say, "I love you," without anyone overhearing him, except d'Artagnan, who followed him, and M. Fouquet, who preceded him.

The night of magical enchantments stole on. The King having requested to be shown his room, there was immediately a movement in every direction. The Queen-Mother and the Queen passed to their own apartments, accompanied by the music of theorbos and lutes; the King found his musketeers awaiting him on the grand flight of steps, for M. Fouquet had brought them on from Mélun, and had invited them to supper. D'Artagnan's suspicions at once disappeared. He was weary, he had supped well, and wished, for once in his life, thoroughly to enjoy a fête given by a man who was in every sense of the word a king. "M. Fouquet," he said, "is the man for me."

The King was conducted with the greatest ceremony to the chamber of Morpheus, of which we owe some slight description to our readers. It was the handsomest and the

largest in the palace. Lebrun had painted on the vaulted
ceiling the happy, as well as disagreeable dreams with which
Morpheus affects kings as well as other men. Everything
that sleep gives birth to that is lovely, its perfumes, its flowers, and nectar, the wild voluptuousness or deep repose of
the senses, had the painter enriched with his frescoes. It
was a composition as soft and pleasing in one part as dark
and gloomy and terrible in another. The poisoned chalice,
the glittering dagger suspended over the head of the sleep-
er; wizards and phantoms with hideous masks, those half-
dim shadows more terrific than the brightness of flame or
the blackness of night; these, and such as these, he had made
the companions of his more pleasing pictures. No sooner
had the King entered the room than a cold shiver seemed to
pass through him, and on Fouquet asking him the cause of
it, the King replied, as pale as death,—

"I am sleepy, that is all."

"Does your Majesty wish for your attendants at once?"

"No; I have to talk with a few persons first," said the
King. "Will you have the goodness to tell M. Colbert I wish
to see him." Fouquet bowed and left the room. It was but
one more indication to him that M. Colbert was replacing
him in the King's affections.

10

High Treason

Doubtless the King was dreaming, and in his dream the crown of gold, which fastened the curtains together, seemed to recede from his vision, just as the dome, to which it remained suspended, had done, so that the winged genius which, with both its hands, supported the crown, seemed, though vainly so, to call upon the King, who was fast disappearing from it. The bed still sank. Louis, with his eyes open, could not resist the deception of this cruel hallucination. At last, as the light of the royal chamber faded away into darkness and gloom, something cold, gloomy, and inexplicable in its nature seemed to infect the air. No paintings, nor gold, nor velvet hangings, were visible any longer, nothing but walls of a dull grey colour, which the increasing gloom made darker every moment. And yet the bed still continued to descend, and after a minute, which seemed in its duration almost an age to the King, it reached a stratum of air, black and still as death, and then it stopped. The King could no longer see the light in his room, except as from the bottom of a well we can see the light of day. "I am under the influence of a terrible dream," he thought. "It is time to awaken from it. Come! Let me wake up."

Every one has experienced what the above remark conveys; there is hardly a person who, in the midst of a nightmare whose influence is suffocating, has not said to himself, by the help of that light which still burns in the brain when every human light is extinguished, "It is nothing but a dream after all." This was precisely what Louis XIV said to himself; but when he said, "Come, come! wake up," he perceived that not only was he already awake, but still more, that he had his eyes open also; he then looked all round him. On his right hand and on his left two armed men stood silently, each wrapped in a huge cloak and the face covered with a mask; one of them held a small lamp in his hand, whose glimmering light revealed the saddest picture a King could look upon. Louis could not help saying to himself that his dream still lasted, and that all he had to do to cause it to disappear was to move his arms or to say something aloud; he darted from his bed, and found himself upon the damp moist ground. Then, addressing himself to the man who held the lamp in his hand, he said,—

"What is this, monsieur, and what is the meaning of this jest?"

"It is no jest," replied in a deep voice the masked figure that held the lantern.

"Do you belong to M. Fouquet?" inquired the King, greatly astonished at his situation.

"It matters very little to whom we belong," said the phantom; "we are your masters now; that is sufficient."

The King, more impatient than intimidated, turned to the other masked figure. "If this is a comedy," he said, "you will tell M. Fouquet that I find it unseemly and improper, and that I desire it should cease."

The second masked person to whom the King had addressed himself was a man of huge stature and vast circumference. He held himself erect and motionless as a block of marble. "Well," added the King, stamping his foot, "you do not answer!"

"We do not answer you, my good monsieur," said the giant in a stentorian voice, "because there is nothing to answer."

"At least tell me what you want?" exclaimed Louis, folding his arms with a passionate gesture.

"You will know by-and-by," replied the man who held the lamp.

"In the meantime tell me where I am."

"Look."

Louis looked all around him; but, by the light of the lamp which the masked figure raised for the purpose, he could perceive nothing but the damp walls which glistened here and there with the slimy traces of the snail. "Oh! Oh, a dungeon!" said the King.

"No, a subterranean passage."

"Which leads—"

"Will you be good enough to follow us?"

"I shall not stir from hence!" cried the King.

"If you are obstinate, my dear young friend," replied the taller and stouter of the two, "I will lift you up in my arms, will roll you up in a cloak, and if you are stifled there, why, so much the worse for you."

And as he said this he disengaged from beneath his cloak a hand of which Milo of Crotona would have envied him the possession, on the day when he had that unhappy idea of rending his last oak. The King dreaded violence, for he could well believe that the two men into whose power he had fallen had not gone so far with any idea of drawing back, and that they would consequently be ready to proceed to extremities, if necessary. He shook his head, and said: "It seems I have fallen into the hands of a couple of assassins. Move on, then."

Neither of the men answered a word to this remark. The one who carried the lantern walked first, and the King followed him, while the second masked figure closed the procession. In this manner they passed along a winding gallery of some length, with as many staircases leading out of it as are to be found in the mysterious and gloomy palaces of Ann Radcliffe's creation. All these windings and turnings, during which the King heard the sound of falling water over his head, ended at last in a long corridor closed by an iron door. The figure with the lamp opened the door with one of the keys he wore suspended at his girdle, where, during the whole of the time, the King had heard them rattle. As soon as the door was opened and admitted the air, Louis recognised the balmy odours which are exhaled by the trees after a hot summer's day. He paused, hesitatingly, for a moment or two; but his huge companion who followed him thrust him out of the subterranean passage.

"Another blow," said the King, turning towards the one who had just had the audacity to touch his sovereign. "What do you intend to do with the King of France?"

"Try to forget that word," replied the man with the lamp, in a tone which as little admitted of a reply as one of the famous decrees of Minos.

"You deserve to be broken on the wheel for the word you have just made use of," said the giant, as he extinguished the lamp his companion handed to him; "but the King is too kind-hearted."

Louis, at the threat, made so sudden a movement, that it seemed as if he meditated flight; but the giant's hand was in a moment placed on his shoulder, and fixed him motionless where he stood. "But tell me, at least, where we are going," said the King.

"Come," replied the former of the two men, with a kind of respect in his manner, and leading his prisoner towards a carriage which seemed to be in waiting.

The carriage was completely concealed amid the trees. Two horses, with their feet fettered, were fastened by a halter to the lower branches of a large oak.

"Get in," said the same man, opening the carriage door, and letting down the step. The King obeyed and seated himself at the back of the carriage, the padded door of which was shut and locked immediately upon him and his guide. As for the giant, he cut the fastenings by which the horses were bound, harnessed them himself, and mounted on the box of the carriage, which was unoccupied. The carriage set off immediately at a quick trot, turned into the road to Paris, and in the forest of Sénart found a relay of horses fastened to trees in the same manner as the first horses had been, and without a postilion. The man on the box changed the horses, and continued to follow the road towards Paris with the same rapidity, and entered the city about three o'clock in the morning. The carriage proceeded along the Faubourg Saint-Antoine, and, after having called out to the sentinel "by the King's order", the driver conducted the horses into the circular enclosure of the Bastille, looking out upon the courtyard, called La Cour du Gouvernement. There the horses drew up, reeking with sweat, at the flight of steps, and a sergeant of the guard ran forward. "Go and wake the governor," said the coachman, in a voice of thunder.

With the exception of this voice, which might have been heard at the entrance of the Faubourg Saint-Antoine, everything remained as calm in the carriage as in the prison. Ten minutes afterwards M. de Baisemeaux appeared in his dressing-gown on the threshold of the door. "What is the matter now?" he asked, "and whom have you brought me there?"

The man with the lantern opened the carriage door, and said two or three words to the one who acted as driver, who immediately got down from his seat, took up a short musket which he kept under his feet, and placed its muzzle on the prisoner's chest.

"And fire at once if he speaks!" added aloud the man who alighted from the carriage.

"Very good!" replied his companion, without any other remark.

With this recommendation, the person who had accompanied the King in the carriage ascended the flight of steps, at the top of which the governor was awaiting him. "Monsieur d'Herblay!" said the latter.

"Hush!" said Aramis. "Let us go into your room."

"Good Heavens! What brings you here at this hour?"

"A mistake, my dear Monsieur de Baisemeaux," Aramis replied quietly. "It appears that you were quite right the other day."

"What about?" inquired the governor.

"About the order of release, my dear friend."

"Tell me what you mean, monsieur—no, monseigneur," said the governor, almost suffocated by surprise and terror.

"It is a very simple affair; you remember, dear M. de Baisemeaux, that an order of release was sent to you."

"Yes, for Marchiali."

Very good! We both thought that it was for Marchiali."

"Certainly; you will recollect, however, that I would not believe it, but that you compelled me."

"Oh, Baisemeaux, my good fellow, what a word to make use of!—strongly recommended, that was all."

"Strongly recommended, yes; strongly recommended to give him up to you: and that you carried him off with you in your carriage."

"Well, my dear Monsieur de Baisemeaux, it was a mistake; it was discovered at the ministry, so that I now bring you an order from the King to set at liberty—Seldon, that poor Scotch fellow, you know."

"Seldon! Are you sure this time?"

"Well, read it yourself," added Aramis, handing him the order.

"Why," said Baisemeaux, "this order is the very same that has already passed through my hands."

"Indeed!"

"It is the very one I assured you I saw the other evening. Rather! I recognise it by the blot of ink."

"I do not know whether it is that or not; but all I know is that I bring it for you."

"But, then, about the other?"

"What other?"

"Marchiali?"

"I have got him here with me."

"But that is not enough for me. I require a new order to take him back again."

"Don't talk such nonsense, my dear Baisemeaux; you talk

like a child! Where is the order you received respecting Marchiali?"

Baisemeaux ran to his iron chest and took it out. Aramis seized hold of it, coolly tore it in four pieces, held them to the lamp, and burnt them. "Good Heaven! what are you doing?" exclaimed Baisémeaux, in an extremity of terror.

"Look at your position a little quietly, my dear governor," said Aramis, with his imperturbable self-possession, "and you will see how very simple the whole affair is. You no longer possess any order justifying Marchiali's release."

"I am a lost man!"

"Far from it, my good fellow, since I have brought Marchiali back to you, and it is just the same as if he had never left."

"Ah!" said the governor, completely overcome by terror.

"Plain enough, you see; and you will go and shut him up immediately."

"I should think so, indeed."

"And you will hand over this Seldon to me, whose liberation is authorised by this order. Do you understand?"

"I—I—"

"You do understand, I see," said Aramis. "Very good."

Baisemeaux clasped his hands together. "But why, at all events, after having taken Marchiali away from me, do you bring him back again?" cried the unhappy governor, in a paroxysm of terror and completely dumbfounded.

"For a friend such as you are," said Aramis, "for so devoted a servant, I have no secrets;" and he put his mouth close to Baisemeaux's ear, as he said in a low tone of voice, "You know the resemblance between that unfortunate fellow and—"

"And the King? Yes!"

"Very good; the very first use that Marchiali made of his liberty was to persist—Can you guess what?"

"How is it likely I should guess?"

"To persist in saying that he was the King of France; to

dress himself up in clothes like those of the King; and then pretend to assume that he was the King himself."

"Gracious Heavens!"

"That is the reason why I have brought him back again, my dear friend. He is mad, and lets every one see how mad he is."

"What is to be done, then?"

"That is very simple; let no one hold any communication with him. You understand, that when his peculiar style of madness came to the King's ears, the King, who had pitied his terrible affliction, and saw how his kindness of heart had been repaid by such black ingratitude, became perfectly furious; so that, now—and remember this very distinctly, dear Monsieur de Baisemeaux, for it concerns you most closely—so that there is now, I repeat, sentence of death pronounced against all those who may allow him to communicate with any one else but me, or the King himself. You understand, Baisemeaux, sentence of death!"

"You need not ask me whether I understand."

"And now let us go down and conduct this poor devil back to his dungeon again, unless you prefer he should come up here."

"What would be the good of that?"

"It would be better, perhaps, to enter his name in the prison-book at once."

"Of course; certainly; not a doubt of it."

"In that case have him up."

Baisemeaux ordered the drums to be beaten, and the bells to be rung, as a warning to every one to retire, in order to avoid meeting a prisoner, about whom it was desired to observe a certain mystery. Then, when the passages were free, he went to take from the carriage the prisoner, at whose breast the huge man, faithful to the direction which had been given him, still kept his musket levelled. "Ah, is that you, miserable wretch?" cried the governor, as soon as he perceived the King. "Very good, very good." And immediately, making the King get out of the carriage, he led him, still accompanied by the giant, who had not taken off his mask, and Aramis, who again resumed his, up the stairs, to the second Bertaudiére, and opened the door of the room in which Philippe for six long years had bemoaned his existence. The King entered into the cell without pronouncing a single word; he was pale and haggard. Baisemeaux shut the door upon him, turned the key twice in the lock, and then returned to Aramis. "It is quite true," he said in a low tone, "that he has a rather strong resemblance to the King; but still, less so than you said."

"So that," said Aramis, "you would not have been deceived by the substitution of the one for the other?"

"What a question!"

"You are a most valuable fellow, Baisemeaux," said Aramis; "and now, set Seldon free."

"Oh, yes. I was going to forget that. I will go and give orders at once."

"Bah! tomorrow will be time enough."

"Tomorrow!"—oh, no. This very minute."

"Well; go off to your own affairs, I shall go away to mine. But it is quite understood, is it not?"

"What is quite understood?"

"That no one is to enter the prisoner's cell, except with an order from the King; an order which I will myself bring."

"Quite so. *Adieu*, monseigneur."

Aramis turned to his companion and addressed him by name. "Now, Porthos, my good fellow, back again to Vaux, and as fast as possible."

"A man is light and easy enough, when he has faithfully served his King; and, in serving him, saved his country," said Porthos. "The horses will be as light as if they had nothing at all behind them. So let us be off." And the carriage, lightened of a prisoner, who might well be—as he in fact was—very very heavy for Aramis, passed across the drawbridge of the Bastille, which was raised again immediately behind it.

11

A Night At The Bastille

When the young King, stupefied and crushed in every sense and feeling, found himself led to a cell in the Bastille, he fancied that death itself is but a sleep; that it, too, has its dreams as well; that the bed had broken through the flooring of his room at Vaux; that death had resulted from the occurrence; and that, still carrying out his dream, as the King, Louis XIV, now no longer living, was dreaming one of those horrors, impossible to realise in life, which is termed dethronement, imprisonment, and insult towards a sovereign, who formerly wielded unlimited power. To be present at—an actual witness, too—of this bitterness of death; to float indecisively, in an incomprehensible mystery, between resemblance and reality; to hear everything, to see everything, without interfering with a single detail of agonising suffering, was—so the King thought within himself—a torture far more terrible, since it might last for ever. "Is this what is termed eternity—hell?" he murmured, at the moment the door closed upon him, which Baisemeaux had himself shut. He did not even look round him; and in the room, leaning with his back against the wall, he allowed himself to be carried away by the terrible supposition that he was already dead, as he closed his eyes in order to avoid looking upon something even worse still. "How can I have died?" he said to himself, sick with terror. "The bed might have been let down by some artificial means? But no! I do not remember to have received any contusion, nor any shock either. Would they not rather have poisoned me at one of

72

my meals, or with the fumes of wax, as they did my ances-
tress, Jeanne d'Albret?" Suddenly, the chill of the dungeon
seemed to fall like a cloak upon Louis's shoulders. "I have
seen," he said, "my father lying dead upon his funeral couch,
in his regal robes. That pale face, so calm and worn, those
hands, once so skilful, lying nerveless by his side; those
limbs stiffened by the icy grasp of death; nothing there be-
tokened a sleep peopled with dreams. And yet, how numerous were the dreams which Heaven might have sent that
royal corpse—him, whom so many others had preceded,
hurried away by him into eternal death! No, that King was
still the King; he was enthroned still upon that funeral couch,
as upon a velvet arm-chair; he had not abdicated aught of
his majesty. God, who had not punished him, cannot, will
not punish me, who have done nothing." A strange sound
attracted the young man's attention. He looked round him,
and saw on the mantel-shelf, just below an enormous crucifix, coarsely painted in fresco on the wall, a rat of enormous size engaged in nibbling a piece of dry bread, but
fixing, all the time, an intelligent and inquiring look upon
the new occupant of the cell. The King could not resist a
sudden impulse of fear and disgust; he moved back towards
the door uttering a loud cry; and, as if he had but needed
this cry, which escaped from his breast almost unconscious-
ly, to recognise himself, Louis knew that he was alive and
in full possession of his natural senses. "A prisoner!" he
cried. "I—I, a prisoner!" He looked round him for a bell to
summon some one to him. "There are no bells at the
Bastille," he said, "and it is in the Bastille I am imprisoned.
In what way can I have been made a prisoner? It must have
been owing to a conspiracy of M. Fouquet. I have been
drawn to Vaux, as into a snare. M. Fouquet cannot be acting alone in this affair. His agent— That voice I but just
now heard was M. d'Herblay's; I recognised it. Colbert was
right, then. But what is Fouquet's object? To reign in my
place and stead?—Impossible. Yet, who knows!" thought

the King, relapsing into gloom again. "Perhaps my brother, the Duc d'Orléans, is doing that which my uncle wished to do during the whole of his life against my father. But the Queen?—My mother, too? And La Vallière? Dear, dear girl! Yes, it is—it must be so. They must have shut her up, as they have me. We are separated for ever!" And at this idea of separation, the poor lover burst into a flood of tears and sobs and groans.

"There is a governor in this place," the King continued, in a fury of passion; "I will speak to him, I will summon him to me."

He called, but no voice replied to his. He seized hold of his chair, and hurled it against the massive oaken door. The wood resounded against the door, and awakened many a mournful echo in the profound depths of the staircase: but from a human creature, not one.

This was a fresh proof for the King of the slight regard in which he was held at the Bastille. Therefore, when his first fit of anger had passed away, having remarked a barred window, through which there passed a stream of light, lozenge-shaped, which must be, he knew, the bright orb of approaching day, Louis began to call out, at first gently enough, then louder and louder still; but no one replied to him. Twenty other attempts which he made, one after another, obtained no other or better success. His blood began to boil within him, and mount to his head. His nature was such, that, accustomed to command, he trembled at the idea of disobedience. By degrees, his anger increased more and more. The prisoner broke the chair, which was too heavy for him to lift, and made use of it as a battering ram to strike against the door. He struck so loudly, and so repeatedly, that the perspiration soon began to pour down his face. The sound became tremendous and continuous; some stifled, smothered cries replied in different directions. This sound produced a strange effect upon the King. He paused to listen to it; it was the voices of the prisoners, formerly his victims, now his companions. The voices ascended like vapours through the thick ceilings and the massive walls, and rose in accusation against the author of this noise, as doubtless their sighs and tears accused, in whispered tones, the author of their captivity. After having deprived so many people of their liberty, the King came among them to rob them of their rest. This idea almost drove him n.ad; it redoubled his strength, or rather his will, bent upon obtaining some information, or a conclusion to the affair. With a portion of the broken chair he recommenced the noise. At the end of an hour, Louis heard something in the corridor, behind the door of his cell, and a violent blow, which was returned upon the door itself, made him cease his own.

"Are you mad?" said a rude brutal voice. "What is the matter with you this morning?"

"This morning!" thought the King; but he said aloud, politely, "Monsieur, are you the governor of the Bastille?"

"My good fellow, your head is out of sorts," replied the voice; "but that is no reason why you should make such a terrible disturbance. Be quiet; curse it!"

"Are you the governor?" the King inquired again.

He heard a door on the corridor close; the jailer had just left, not even condescending to reply a single word. When the King had assured himself of this departure, his fury knew no longer any bounds. As agile as a tiger, he leaped from the table to the window, and struck the iron bars with all his might. He broke a pane of glass, the pieces of which fell clanking into the courtyard below. He shouted with increasing hoarseness, "The governor, the governor!" This excess lasted fully an hour, during which time he was in a burning fever. With his hair in disorder and matted on his forehead, his dress torn and whitened, his linen in shreds, the King never rested until his strength was utterly exhausted, and it was not until then that he clearly understood the pitiless thickness of the walls, the impenetrable nature of the cement, invincible to all other influence but that of time, and possessed of no other weapon but despair. He leaned his forehead against the door, and let the feverish throbbings of his heart calm by degrees; it seemed as if one single additional pulsation would have made it burst.

"A moment will come when the food which is given to the prisoners will be brought to me. I shall then see some one, I shall speak to him, and get an answer."

And the King tried to remember at what hour the first repast of the prisoners was served at the Bastille; he was ignorant even of this detail. The feeling of remorse at this remembrance smote him like the keen thrust of a dagger, that he should have lived for five-and-twenty years a King, and in the enjoyment of every happiness, without having bestowed a moment's thought on the misery of those who had been unjustly deprived of their liberty. The King blushed from very shame. He felt that Heaven, in permitting this fearful humiliation, did no more than render to the man the same torture as was inflicted by that man upon so many others. Nothing could be more efficacious for reawakening his mind to religious influences than the prostration of his heart and mind and soul beneath the feelings of such acute wretchedness. But Louis dared not even kneel in prayer to God to entreat Him to terminate his bitter trial.

"Heaven is right," he said; "Heaven acts wisely, it would be cowardly to pray to Heaven for that which I have so often refused to my own fellow creatures."

He had reached this stage of his reflection, that is, of his agony of mind, when a similar noise was again heard behind his door, followed this time by the sound of the key in the lock, and of the bolts being withdrawn from their staples. The King bounded forward to be nearer to the person who was about to enter, but suddenly reflecting that it was a movement unworthy of a sovereign, he paused, assumed a noble and calm expression, which for him was easy enough, and waited with his back turned towards the window, in order, to some extent, to conceal his agitation from the eyes of the person who was about entering. It was only a jailer with a basket of provisions. The King looked at the man with restless anxiety, and waited until he spoke.

"Ah!" said the latter, "you have broken your chair. I said you had done so. Why, you must have become quite mad."

"Monsieur," said the King, "be careful what you say; it will be a very serious affair for you."

The jailer placed the basket on the table, and looked at his prisoner steadily. "What do you say?" he said.

"Desire the governor to come to me," added the King, in accents full of dignity.

"Come, my boy," said the turnkey, "you have always been very quiet and reasonable, but you are getting vicious, it seems, and I wish you to know it in time. You have broken your chair, and made a great disturbance; that is an offence punishable by imprisonment in one of the lower dungeons. Promise me not to begin over again, and I will not say a word about it to the governor."

"I wish to see the governor," replied the King, still controlling his passion.

"He will send you off to one of the dungeons, I tell you, so take care."

"I insist upon it, do you hear?"

"Ah! ah! your eyes are becoming wild again. Very good! I shall take away your knife."

And the jailer did what he said, quitted the prisoner, and closed the door, leaving the King more astounded, more wretched, and more isolated than ever. M. de Baisemeaux, thoroughly impressed with what Aramis had told him, and in perfect conformity with the King's order, hoped only that one thing might happen; namely, that the madman, Marchiali, might be mad enough to hang himself to the canopy of his bed, or to one of the bars of the window. In fact, the prisoner was anything but a profitable investment for M. Baisemeaux, and became more annoying than agreeable to him. These complications of Seldon and Marchiali—the complications, first of setting at liberty and then imprisoning again, the complications arising from the strong likeness in question—had at last found a very proper *dénouement*. Baisemeaux even thought he had remarked that M. d'Herblay himself was not altogether dissatisfied at it.

"And then, really," said Baisemeaux to his next in command, "an ordinary prisoner is already unhappy enough in being a prisoner; he suffers quite enough, indeed, to induce one to hope, charitably enough, that his death may not be far distant. With still greater reason, then, when the prisoner has gone mad, and might bite and make a terrible disturbance in the Bastille: why, in that case, it is not simply an act of mere charity to wish him dead; it would be almost a good and even commendable action quietly to put him out of his misery."

And the good-natured governor thereupon sat down to his late breakfast.

12

The Morning

In opposition to the sad and terrible destiny of the King imprisoned in the Bastille, and tearing, in sheer despair, the bolts and bars of his dungeon, the rhetoric of the chroniclers of old would not fail to present as a complete antithesis the picture of Philippe lying asleep beneath the royal canopy.

Towards the morning a shadow, rather than a body, glided into the royal chamber. Philippe expected his approach, and neither expressed nor exhibited any surprise.

"Well, M. d'Herblay?" he said.

"Well, sire, all is done."

"How?"

"Exactly as we expected."

"Did he resist?"

"Terribly! Tears and entreaties!"

"And then?"

"A perfect stupor."

"But at last?"

"Oh, at last, a complete victory, and absolute silence."

"Did the governor of the Bastille suspect anything?"

"Nothing."

"The resemblance, however—"

"That was the cause of the success."

"But the prisoner cannot fail to explain himself. Think well of that; I have myself been able to do that on a former occasion."

"I have already provided for everything. In a few days,

sooner, if necessary, we will take the captive out of his prison and will send him out of the country, to a place of exile so remote—"

"People can return from their exile, Monsieur d'Herblay."

"To a place of exile so distant, I was going to say, that human strength and the duration of human life would not be enough for his return."

And once more a cold look of intelligence passed between Aramis and the young King.

"And M. du Vallon, our friend Porthos?" asked Philippe, in order to change the conversation.

"He will be presented to you today, and confidentially will congratulate you on the danger which that conspirator has made you run."

"What is to be done with him?"

"With M. du Vallon?"

"Yes; confer a dukedom on him, I suppose."

"A dukedom," replied Aramis, smiling in a significant manner.

"Why do you laugh, Monsieur d'Herblay?"

"I laugh at the extreme caution of your idea."

"Cautious! Why so?"

"Your Majesty is doubtless afraid that poor Porthos may probably become a troublesome witness, and you wish to get rid of him."

"What! In making him a duke?"

"Certainly; you would assuredly kill him, for he would die from joy, and the secret would die with him."

"Good Heavens!"

"Yes," said Aramis phlegmatically; "I should lose a very good friend."

At this moment, and in the middle of this idle conversation, under the light tone of which the two conspirators concealed their joy and pride at their mutual success, Aramis heard something which made him prick up his ears.

"What is that?" said Philippe.

"The dawn, sire."

"Well?"

"Well, before you retired to bed last night, you probably decided to do something this morning at the break of day."

"Yes, I told d'Artagnan my captain of the musketeers," replied the young man hurriedly, "that I should expect him?"

"If you told him that, he will certainly be here, for he is a most punctual man."

"I hear a step in the vestibule."

"It must be he."

"Come, let us begin the attack," said the young King resolutely.

"Be cautious, for Heaven's sake; to begin the attack, and with d'Artagnan, would be madness. D'Artagnan knows nothing, he has seen nothing; he is a hundred miles from suspecting our mystery in the slightest degree; but if he comes into this room the first this morning, he will be sure to detect something which has taken place, and which he would think his business to occupy himself about. Before we allow d'Artagnan to penetrate into this room, we must air the room thoroughly, or introduce so many people into it, that the keenest scent in the whole kingdom may be deceived by the traces of twenty different persons."

"But how can I send him away, since I have given him a rendezvous?" observed the Prince, impatient to measure swords with so redoubtable an antagonist.

"I will take care of that," replied the Bishop, "and in order to begin, I am going to strike a blow which will completely stupefy our man."

"He too is striking a blow, for I hear him at the door," added the Prince hurriedly.

And, in fact, a knock at the door was heard at that moment. Aramis was not mistaken; for it was indeed d'Artagnan who adopted that mode of announcing himself.

The door opened. The captain thought that it was the King who had just opened it himself; and this supposition was not altogether inadmissible, considering the state of agitation in which he had left Louis XIV the previous evening; but instead of his royal master, whom he was on the point of saluting with the greatest respect, he perceived the long, calm features of Aramis. So extreme was his surprise, that he could hardly refrain from uttering a loud exclamation. "Aramis!" he said.

"Good morning, dear d'Artagnan," replied the prelate coldly.

"You here," stammered the musketeer.

"His Majesty desires you to report that he is still sleeping, after having been greatly fatigued during the whole night."

"Ah!" said d'Artagnan, who could not understand how the Bishop of Vannes, who had been so indifferent a favourite the previous evening, had become in half a dozen hours the largest mushroom of fortune which had ever sprung up in a sovereign's bedroom. In fact, to transmit the orders of the King even to the mere threshold of that monarch's room, to serve as an intermediary of Louis XIV, so as to be able to give a single order in his name at a couple of paces from him, he must be greater than Richelieu had ever been to Louis XIII. D'Artagnan's expressive eye, his half-opened lips, his curling moustache, said as much indeed, in the plainest language to the chief favourite who remained calm and perfectly unmoved.

"Moreover," continued the Bishop, "you will be good enough, captain, to allow those only to pass into the King's room this morning who have special permission. His Majesty does not wish to be disturbed just yet."

"But," objected d'Artagnan, almost on the point of refusing to obey this order, and particularly of giving unrestrained passage to the suspicions which the King's silence had aroused—" but, my Lord Bishop, His Majesty gave me a rendezvous for this morning."

"Later, later," said the King's voice, from the bottom of

the alcove; a voice which made a cold shudder pass through the musketeer's veins. He bowed, amazed, confuted, and stupefied by the smile with which Aramis seemed to overwhelm him, as soon as those words had been pronounced.

13

The King's Friend

Fouquet was waiting with anxiety; the King's growing distrust of him in favour of M. Colbert worried him deeply. He had already sent away many of his servants and his friends, who, anticipating the usual hour of his ordinary receptions, had called at his door to inquire after him. Preserving the utmost silence respecting the danger which hung suspended over his head, he only asked them, as he did every one indeed who came to the door, where Aramis was. When he saw d'Artagnan return, and when he perceived the Bishop of Vannes behind him, he could hardly restrain his delight; it was fully equal to his previous uneasiness. The mere sight of Aramis was a complete compensation to the Superintendant for the unhappiness he had undergone. The prelate was silent and grave; d'Artagnan completely bewildered by such an accumulation of events.

"Well, captain; so you have brought M. d'Herblay to me."

"But you," said d'Artagnan, adressing Aramis, "you who have become M. Fouquet's protector and patron, can you not do something for me?"

"Anything you like, my friend," replied the Bishop, in a calm voice.

"One thing only, then, and I shall be perfectly satisfied. How have you managed to become the favourite of the King, you who have never spoken to him more than twice in your life?"

"From a friend such as you are," said Aramis, "I cannot conceal anything."

"From a friend such as you are," said Aramis, "I cannot conceal anything."

"Ah, very good; tell me, then."

"Very well. You think that I have seen the King only twice, while the fact is I have seen him more than a hundred times; only we have kept it very secret, that is all." And without trying to remove the colour which at this revelation made d'Artagnan's face flush scarlet, Aramis turned towards M. Fouquet, who was as much surprised as the musketeer. "Monseigneur," he resumed, "the King desires me to inform you that he is more than ever your friend and that your beautiful fête, so generously offered by you on his behalf, has touched him to the very heart."

And thereupon he saluted M. Fouquet with so much reverence of manner, that the latter, incapable of understanding a man whose diplomacy was of so prodigious a character, remained incapable of uttering a single syllable, and equally incapable of thought or movement. D'Artagnan fancied he perceived that these two men had something to say to each other, and he was about to yield to that feeling of instinctive politeness which in such a case hurries a man towards the door, when he feels his presence is an an inconvenience for others; but his eager curiosity, spurred on by so many mysteries, counselled him to remain.

Aramis thereupon turned towards him and said in a quiet tone, "You will not forget, my friend, the King's order respecting those whom he intends to receive this morning on rising." These words were clear enough, and the musketeer understood them; he, therefore, bowed to Fouquet and then to Aramis,—to the latter with a slight admixture of ironical respect,—and disappeared.

No sooner had he left, than Fouquet, whose impatience had hardly been able to wait for that moment, darted towards the door to close it, and then returning to the Bishop, he said, "My dear d'Herblay, I think it now high time you should explain to me what has passed, for, in plain and honest truth, I do not understand anything."

"We will explain all that to you," said Aramis, sitting down and making Fouquet sit down also. "Where shall I begin?"

"With this, first of all. Why is the King now so favourably disposed to me?"

"You ought rather to ask me what was his reason for having had suspicions of you."

"Since last night, I have had time to think over it, and my idea is that it arises out of some slight feeling of jealousy. My fête put M. Colbert out of temper, and M. Colbert discovered some cause of complaint against me; Belle-Isle, my fortified island, for instance."

"No; there is no question at all just now of Belle-Isle."

"What is it, then?"

"Do you remember those receipts for thirteen millions which M. de Mazarin contrived to get stolen from you?"

"Yes, of course!"

"Well, you are already pronounced to be a public robber."

"Good heavens!"

"Alas, yes!"

"And that proclaims you a traitor and suborner."

"Why should he have pardoned me, then?"

"We have not yet arrived at that part of our argument. I wish you to be quite convinced of the fact itself. Observe this well: the King knows you to be guilty of an appropriation of public funds. Oh, of course I know that you have done nothing of the kind; but, at all events, the King has not seen the receipts, and he cannot do otherwise than believe you criminal."

"I beg your pardon; I do not see—"

"You will see presently, though. The King, moreover, having read your love-letter to La Vallière, and the offers you there made her, cannot retain any doubt of your intentions with regard to that young lady; you will admit that, I suppose?"

"Certainly. But, conclude."

"In a few words. The King is, therefore, a powerful, implacable, and eternal enemy for you."

"Agreed. But am I, then, so powerful that he has not dared to sacrifice me, notwithstanding his hatred, with all the means which my weakness, or my misfortunes, may have given him as a hold upon me."

"It is clear, beyond all doubt," pursued Aramis coldly, "that the King has quarrelled irreconcilably with you."

"But, since he absolves me—"

"Do you believe it likely?" asked the Bishop, with a searching look.

"Without believing in his sincerity of heart, I believe in the truth of the fact."

Aramis slightly shrugged his shoulders.

"But why, then, should Louis XIV have commissioned you to tell me what you have just stated?"

"The King charged me with nothing for you.... Oh, yes. You are quite right. There is an order, certainly." These words were pronounced by Aramis in so strange a tone, that Fouquet could not resist starting.

"You are concealing something from me, I see. What is it?'

Aramis softly rubbed his white fingers over his chin, but said nothing.

"Does the King exile me?"

"Do not act as if you were playing at the game children play at when they have to try to guess where a thing has been hidden, and are informed by a bell being rung, when they are approaching near to it, or going away from it."

"Speak then."

"Guess."

"You alarm me."

"Bah! That is because you have not guessed, then."

"What did the King say to you? In the name of our friendship, do not deceive me."

"The King has not said a word to me."

" You are killing me with impatience, d'Herblay. Am I still Superintendant?"

"As long as you like."

"But what extraordinay empire have you so suddenly acquired over His Majesty's mind?"

"Ah, that is it."

"You make him do as you like."

"I believe so."

"It is hardly credible."

"So any one would say."

"D'Herblay, by our alliance, by our friendship, by everything you hold dearest in the world, speak openly, I implore you. By what means have you succeeded in overcoming Louis XIV's prejudices, for he did not like you, I know?"

"The King will like me *now*," said Aramis, laying a stress upon the last word.

"You have something particular then, between you?"

"Yes."

"A secret, perhaps?"

"Yes, a secret."

"A secret of such a nature as to change his Majesty's interests?"

"You are, indeed, a man of superior intelligence, monseigneur, and have made a very accurate guess. I have, in fact, discovered a secret, of a nature to change the interests of the King of France."

"Ah!" said Fouquet, with the reserve of a man who does not wish to ask any questions.

"And you shall judge of it yourself," pursued Aramis; "and you shall tell me if I am mistaken with regard to the importance of this secret."

"I am listening, since you are good enough to unbosom yourself to me; only do not forget that I have asked you nothing which may be indiscreet in you to communicate."

Aramis seemed, for a moment, as if he were collecting himself.

"Do not speak!" said Fouquet; "there is still time enough."

"Do you remember," said the Bishop, casting down his eyes, "the birth of Louis XIV?"

"As it were yesterday."

"Have you heard anything particular respecting his birth?"

"Nothing; except that the King was not really the son of Louis XIII."

"That does not matter to us, or the kingdom either; he is the son of his father, says the French law, whose father is recognised by the law."

"True; but it is a grave matter, when the quality of races is called into question."

"A merely secondary question, after all. So that, in fact, you have never learned or heard anything in particular?"

"Nothing."

"That is where my secret begins. The Queen, you must know, instead of being delivered of one son, was delivered of two children."

Fouquet looked up suddenly, as he replied, "And the second is dead?"

"You will see. These twins seemed likely to be regarded as the pride of their mother, and the hope of France; but the weak nature of the King, his superstitious feelings, made him apprehend a series of conflicts between two children whose rights were equal; and so he put out of the way—he suppressed— one of the twins."

"Suppressed, do you say?"

"Be patient. Both the children grew up: the one on the throne, whose minister you are; the other, who is my friend, in gloom and isolation."

"Good Heavens! What are you saying, Monsieur d'Herblay? And what is this poor Prince doing?"

"Ask me rather, what he has done."

"Yes, yes."

"He was brought up in the country, and then thrown into a fortress which goes by the name of the Bastille."

"Is it possible?" cried the Surintendant, clasping his hands.

"The one was the most fortunate of men; the other the most unhappy and most miserable of all living beings."

"Does his mother not know this?"

"Anne of Austria knows it all."

"And the King?"

"Knows absolutely nothing."

"So much the better!" said Fouquet.

This remark seemed to make a great impression on Aramis; he looked at Fouquet with the most anxious expression of countenance.

"I beg your pardon; I interrupted you," said Fouquet.

"I was saying," resumed Aramis, "that this poor Prince was the unhappiest of human beings, when Heaven, whose thoughts are over all His creatures, undertook to come to his assistance."

"Oh! in what way? Tell me!"

"You will see. The reigning King—I say the reigning King—you can guess very well why?"

"No. Why?"

"Because both of them, being legitimately entitled from their birth, ought to have been kings. Is not that your opinion?"

"It is, certainly."

"Unreservedly so?"

"Most unreservedly; twins are one person in two bodies."

"I am pleased that a legist of your learning and authority should have pronounced such an opinion. It is agreed, then, that both of them possessed the same rights, is it not?"

"Incontestably so! But, gracious Heaven, what an extraordinary circumstance."

"We are not at the end of it yet. Patience."

"Oh! I shall find patience enough."

"Heaven wished to raise up for that oppressed child an avenger, or a supporter, or vindicator, if you prefer it. It happened that the reigning King, the usurper—(you are quite of my opinion, I believe, that it is an act of usurpation quietly to enjoy, and selfishly to assume the right over, an inheritance to which a man has only the right of one half?)—"

"Yes, usurpation is the word."

"In that case, I continue. It was Heaven's will that the usurper should possess, in the person of his first minister, a man of great talent, of large and generous nature."

"Well, well," said Fouquet, "I understand; you have relied upon me to repair the wrong which has been done to this unhappy brother of Louis XIV. You have thought well; I will help you. I thank you, d'Herblay, I thank you."

"Oh, no, it is not that at all; you have not allowed me to finish," said Aramis, perfectly unmoved.

"I will not say another word, then."

"M. Fouquet, I was observing, the minister of the reigning sovereign was suddenly taken into the greatest aversion, and menaced with the ruin of his fortune, with loss of liberty, with loss of life even, by M. Colbert's intrigue and personal hatred, to which the King gave too readily an attentive ear. But Heaven permits (still, however, out of consideration for the unhappy Prince who had been sacrificed) that M. Fouquet should in his turn have a devoted friend who knew this state secret, and felt that he possessed strength and courage enough to divulge this secret, after having had the strength to carry it locked up in his own heart for twenty years."

"Do not go on any further," said Fouquet, full of generous feelings. "I understand you, and can guess everything now. You went to see the King when his suspicions and distrust reached you; you implored him, he refused to listen to you; then you threatened him with that secret, threatened to reveal it, and Louis XIV, alarmed at the risk of its betrayal, granted to the terror of your indiscretion what he refused to your generous intercession. I understand, I understand: you have the King in your power; I understand."

"You understand nothing as yet," replied Aramis, "and again you have interrupted me. And then, too, allow me to observe that you pay no attention to logical reasoning, and seem to forget what you ought most to remember."

"What do you mean?"

"You know upon what I laid the greatest stress at the beginning of our conversation?"

"Yes; His Majesty's hate, invincible hate for me—yes; but what feeling of hate could resist the threat of such a revelation?"

"Such a revelation, do you say? That is the very point where your logic fails you. What! Do you suppose that if I had made such a revelation to the King, I should have been alive now?"

"It is not ten minutes ago since you were with the King."

"That may be. He might not have had the time to get me killed outright, but he would have had the time to get me gagged and thrown into a dungeon. Come, come, show a little consistency in your reasoning, *mordioux* !"

And by the mere use of this word, which was so thoroughly his old musketeer's expression, forgotten by one who never seemed to forget anything, Fouquet could not but understand to what a pitch of exaltation the calm, impenetrable Bishop of Vannes had wrought himself. He shuddered at it.

"And then," replied the latter, after having mastered his feelings, "should I be the man I really am, should I be the true friend you regard me as, if I were to expose you, you whom the King hates already bitterly enough, to a feeling still more than ever to be dreaded in that young man? To have robbed him is nothing; to have addressed the woman he loves is not much; but to hold in your keeping both his crown and his honour, why, he would rather pluck out your heart with his own hands."

"You have not allowed him to penetrate your secret, then?"

"I would sooner, far sooner, have swallowed at one draught all the poisons that Mithridates drank in twenty years, in order to try to avoid death, than have betrayed my secret to the King."

"What have you done, then?"

"Ah, now we are coming to the point, monseigneur. I think I shall not fail to excite a little interest in you. You are listening, I hope?"

"How can you ask me if I am listening? Go on."

Aramis walked softly all round the room, satisfied himself that they were alone, and that all was silent, and then returned and placed himself close to the arm-chair in which Fouquet was seated, awaiting with the deepest anxiety the revelations he had to make.

"I forgot to tell you," resumed Aramis, addressing himself to Fouquet, who listened to him with the most absorbed attention—"I forgot to mention a most remarkable circumstance respecting these twins, namely, that God had formed them so startlingly, so miraculously, like each other, that it would be utterly impossible to distinguish the one from the other. Their own mother would not be able to distinguish them."

"Is it possible?" exclaimed Fouquet.

"The same noble character in their features, the same carriage, the same stature, the same voice."

"But their thoughts? Degree of intelligence? Their knowledge of human life?"

"There is inequality there, I admit, monseigneur. Yes; for the prisoner of the Bastille is, most incontestably, superior in every way to his brother, and if, from his prison, this unhappy victim were to pass to the throne, France would not, from the earliest period of its history, perhaps, have had a master more powerful by his genius and true nobleness of character."

Fouquet buried his face in his hands, as if he were overwhelmed by the weight of this immense secret. Aramis approached him.

"There is a further inequality," he said, continuing his work of temptation, "an inequality which concerns yourself, monseigneur, between the twins, both sons of Louis XIII, namely, the last-comer does not know M. Colbert."

Fouquet raised his head immediately; his features were pale and distorted. The bolt had hit its mark—not his heart, but his mind and comprehension.

"I understand you," he said to Aramis; "you are proposing a conspiracy to me?"

"Something like it."

"One of these attempts, which, as you said at the beginning of this conversation, alters the fate of empires?"

"And of the Superintendant too—yes, monseigneur."

"In a word, you propose that I should agree to the substitution of the son of Louis XIII, who is now a prisoner in the Bastille, for the son of Louis XIII, who is now at this moment asleep in the Chamber of Morpheus?"

Aramis smiled with the sinister expression of the sinister thought which was passing through his brain, "Exactly," he said.

"Have you thought," continued Fouquet, becoming animated with that strength of talent which in a few seconds originates and matures the conception of a plan, and with that largeness of view which foresees all its consequences, and embraces all its results at a glance—"have you thought that we must assemble the nobility, the clergy, and the third estate of the realm; that we shall have to depose the reigning sovereign, to disturb by so frightful a scandal the tomb of their dead father, to sacrifice the life, the honour of a woman, Anne of Austria, the life and peace of mind of another woman, Maria Theresa; and suppose that all were done, if we succeed in doing it—"

"I do not understand you," continued Aramis slowly. "There is not a single word of the slightest use in what you have just said."

"What!" said the Superintendant, surprised. "A man like you refuse to view the practical bearings of the case! Do you confine yourself to the childish delight of a political illusion, and neglect the chances of its being carried into execution; in other words, the reality itself. Is it possible?"

"My friend," said Aramis, emphasising the word with a kind of disdainful familiarity, "what does Heaven do in order to substitute one king for another?"

"Heaven!" exclaimed Fouquet. "Heaven gives directions to its agent, who seizes upon the doomed victim, hurries him away, and seats the triumphant rival on the empty throne. But you forget that this agent is called death. Oh; Monsieur d'Herblay, in Heaven's name, tell me if you have had the idea—"

"There is no question of that, monseigneur; you are going beyond the object in view. Who spoke of Louis XIV's death? Who spoke of adopting the example which Heaven sets in following out the strict execution of its decrees? No; I wish you to understand that Heaven effects its purposes without confusion or disturbance, without exciting comment or remark, without difficulty or exertion; and that men inspired by Heaven succeed like Heaven itself in all their undertakings, in all they attempt, in all they do."

"What do you mean?"

"I mean, my *friend*," returned Aramis, with the same intonation on the word "friend" that he had applied to it the first time—"I mean that if there has been any confusion, scandal, and even effort in the substitution of the prisoner for the King, I defy you to prove it."

"What!" cried Fouquet, whiter than the handkerchief with which he wiped his temples. "What do you say?"

"Go to the King's apartment," continued Aramis tranquilly, "and you who know the mystery, I defy even you to perceive that the prisoner of the Bastille is lying in his brother's bed."

"But the King?" stammered Fouquet, seized with horror at the intelligence.

"What King?" said Aramis, in his gentlest tone; "the one who hates you, or the one who likes you?"

"The King—of yesterday."

"The King of yesterday! Be quite easy on that score; he

has gone to take the place in the Bastille which his victim has occupied for such a long time past."

"Great God! And who took him there?"

"I."

"You!"

"Yes, and in the simplest way. I carried him away last night from the chamber of Morpheus into a subterranean passage; and while he was descending into gloom, the other was ascending into light. I do not think there has been any disturbance created in any way. A flash of lightning without thunder never awakens any one."

Fouquet uttered a thick, smothered cry, as if he had been struck by some invisible blow, and clasping his head between his clenched hands, he murmured: "You did that?"

"Cleverly enough, too; what do you think of it?"

"You dethroned the King? Imprisoned him, too?"

"Yes, that has been done."

"And such an action has been committed here at Vaux?"

"Yes, here, at Vaux, in the Chamber of Morpheus. It would almost seem that it had been built in anticipation of such an act."

"And at what time did it occur?"

"Last night, between twelve and one o'clock."

Fouquet made a movement as if he were on the point of springing upon Aramis; he restrained himself. "At Vaux! Under my roof!" he said, in a half-strangled voice.

"I believe so; for it is still your house, and is likely to continue so, since M. Colbert cannot rob you of it now."

"It was under my roof, then, monsieur, that you committed this crime?"

"This crime!" said Aramis stupefied.

"This abominable crime!" pursued Fouquet, becoming more and more excited. "This crime more execrable than an assassination! This crime which dishonours my name for ever, and entails upon me the horror of posterity!"

"You are not in your senses, monsieur," replied Aramis,

in an irresolute tone of voice; "you are speaking too loudly; take care!"

"I will call out so loudly that the whole world shall hear me."

"Monsieur Fouquet, take care."

Fouquet turned round towards the prelate, whom he looked at full in the face. "You have dishonoured me," he said, "in committing so foul an act of treason, so heinous a crime upon my guest, upon one who was peacefully reposing beneath my roof. Oh! woe, woe, is me!"

"Woe to the man, rather, who beneath your roof meditated the ruin of your fortune, your life. Do you forget that?"

"He was my guest, my sovereign."

Aramis rose, his eyes literally bloodshot, his mouth trembling convulsively. "Have I a man out of his senses to deal with?" he said.

"You have an honourable man to deal with."

"You are mad."

"A man who will prevent you consummating your crime."

"You are mad, I say."

"A man who would sooner, oh, far sooner, die; who would kill you, even, rather than allow you to complete his dishonour."

And Fouquet snatched up his sword, which d'Artagnan had placed at the head of his bed, and clenched it resolutely in his hand. Aramis frowned, and thrust his hand into his breast as if in search of a weapon. This movement did not escape Fouquet, who, full of nobleness and pride in his magnanimity, threw his sword to a distance from him, and approached Aramis so close as to touch his shoulder with his disarmed hand. "Monsieur," he said, "I would sooner die here on the spot than survive this terrible disgrace; and if you have any pity left for me, I entreat you to take my life."

Aramis remained silent and motionless.

"You do not reply?" said Fouquet.

Aramis raised his head gently, and a glimmer of hope

might be seen once more to animate his eyes. "Reflect, monseigneur," he said, "upon everything we have to expect. As
the matter now stands, the King is still alive, and his imprisonment saves your life."

"Yes," replied Fouquet, "you may have been acting on
my behalf, but I will not, do not accept your services. But,
first of all, I do not wish your ruin. You will leave this house."

Aramis stifled the exclamation which almost escaped his
broken heart.

"I am hospitable towards all who are dwellers beneath
my roof," continued Fouquet, with an air of inexpressible
majesty; "you will not be more fatally lost, than he whose
ruin you have consummated."

"You will be so," said Aramis, in a hoarse, prophetic voice;
"you will be so, believe me."

"I accept the augury, Monsieur d'Herblay; but nothing
shall prevent me, nothing shall stop me. You will leave
Vaux—you must leave France; I give you four hours to place
yourself out of the King's reach."

"Four hours?" said Aramis, scornfully and incredulously.

"Upon the word of Fouquet, no one shall follow you before the expiration of that time. You will therefore have
four hours advance of those whom the King may wish to
despatch after you."

"Four hours!" repeated Aramis, in a thick, smothered voice.

"It is more than you will need to get on board a vessel and
flee to Belle-Isle, which I give you as a place of refuge."

"Ah!" murmured Aramis.

"Belle-Isle is as much mine for you, as Vaux is mine for the
King. Go, d'Herblay, go! As long as I live, not a hair of your
head shall be injured."

"Thank you," said Aramis, with a cold irony of manner.

"Go at once then, and give me your hand, before we both
hasten away; you to save your life, I to save my honour."

Aramis withdrew from his breast the hand he had concealed
there; it was stained with blood. He had dug his nails into his

flesh, as if in punishment for having nursed so many projects, more vain, insensate, and fleeting than the life of man himself. Fouquet was horror-stricken, and then his heart smote him with pity. He threw open his arms as if to embrace him.

"I had no arms," murmured Aramis, as wild and terrible in his wrath as the shade of Dido. And then, without touching Fouquet's hand, he turned his head aside, and stepped back a pace or two. His last word was an imprecation, his last gesture a curse, which his blood-stained hand seemed to invoke, as it sprinkled on Fouquet's face a few drops of blood which flowed from his breast. And both of them darted out of the room by the secret staircase which led down to the inner courtyard. Fouquet ordered his best horses, while Aramis paused at the foot of the staircase which led to Porthos's apartment. He reflected profoundly and for some time, while Fouquet's carriage left the stone-paved courtyard at full gallop.

"Shall I go alone?" said Aramis to himself, "or warn the Prince? Oh, fury! Warn the Prince, and then—do what? Take him with me? To carry this accusing witness about with me everywhere? War, too, would follow—civil war, implacable in its nature! And without any resource to save myself—it is impossible! What could he do without me? Oh, without me he would be utterly destroyed. Yet who knows? Let the destiny be fulfilled—condemned he was, let him remain so then! Good or evil spirit—gloomy and scornful Power, whom men call the Genius of Man, thou art a power more restlessly uncertain, more baselessly useless, than the wild wind in the mountains; Chance thou term'st thyself, but thou art nothing; thou inflamest everything with thy breath, crumblest at the presence of the Cross of dead wood, behind which stands another Power invisible like thyself—whom thou deniest perhaps, but whose avenging hand is on thee, and hurls thee in the dust dishonoured and unnamed! Lost!—I am lost! What can be done? Flee to Belle-Isle? Yes, and leave Porthos behind me, to talk and relate the whole affair to every one! Porthos, too, will have to suffer for what he has done. I will not let poor Porthos suffer. He seems like one of the members of my own frame; and his grief or misfortune would be mine as well. Porthos shall leave with me, and shall follow my destiny. It must be so."

And Aramis, apprehensive of meeting any one to whom his hurried movements might appear suspicious, ascended the staircase without being perceived. Porthos, so recently returned from Paris, was already in a profound sleep; his huge body forgot its fatigue, as his mind forgot its thoughts. Aramis entered, light as a shadow, and placed his nervous grasp on the giant's shoulder. "Come, Porthos," he cried, "come."

Porthos obeyed, rose from his bed, opened his eyes, even before his intelligence seemed to be aroused.

"We are going off," said Aramis.

"Ah!" returned Porthos.

"We shall go mounted, and faster than we have ever gone in our lives."

"Ah!" repeated Porthos.

"Dress yourself, my friend."

And he helped the giant to dress himself, and thrust his gold and diamonds into his pocket. Whilst he was thus engaged, a slight noise attracted his attention, and on looking up he saw d'Artagnan watching them through the half-open door. Aramis started.

"What the devil are you doing there in such an agitated manner?" said the musketeer.

" Hush!" said Porthos.

"We are going off on a mission of great importance," added the Bishop.

"You are very fortunate," said the musketeer.

"Oh, dear me!" said Porthos, "I feel so wearied; I would far sooner have been fast asleep. But the service of the King—"

"Have you seen M. Fouquet?" said Aramis to d'Artagnan.

"Yes, this very minute, in a carriage."

"What did he say to you?"

" '*Adieu*'; nothing more."

"Was that all?"

"What else do you think he could say? Am I worth anything now, since you have all got into such high favour?"

"Listen," said Aramis, embracing the musketeer; "your good times are returning again. You will have no occasion to be jealous of any one."

"Ah, bah!"

"I predict that something will happen to you today which will increase your importance more than ever."

"Really?"

"You know that I know all the news?"

"Oh, yes!"

"Come, Porthos, are you ready? Let us go."

"I am quite ready, Aramis."

"Let us embrace d'Artagnan first."

"Most certainly."

"But the horses?"

"Oh, there is no want of them here. Will you have mine?"

"No; Porthos has his own stud. So *adieu! adieu!*"

The two fugitives mounted their horses beneath the captain of the musketeers' eyes, who held Porthos's stirrup for him, and gazed after them until they were out of sight.

"On any other occasion," thought the Gascon, "I should say that those gentlemen are making their escape; but in these days politics seem so changed that that is what is termed going on a mission. I have no objection; let me attend to my own affairs, that is quite enough;" and he philosophically entered his apartments.

14

Showing How The Countersign Was Respected At The Bastille

Fouquet tore along as fast as his horses could drag him. On his way he trembled with horror at the idea of what had just been revealed to him.

"What must have been," he thought, "the youth of those extraordinary men, who, even as age is stealing fast upon them, still are able to conceive such plans, and can carry them out without flinching?"

At one moment he could not resist the idea that all that Aramis had just been recounting to him was nothing more than a dream, and whether the fable itself was not the snare; so that when Fouquet arrived at the Bastille he might possibly find an order of arrest, which would send him to join the dethroned King. Strongly impressed with this idea, he gave certain sealed orders on his route, while fresh horses were being harnessed to his carriage. These orders were addressed to M. d'Artagnan and to certain others whose fidelity to the King was far above suspicion.

"In this way," said Fouquet to himself, "prisoner or not, I shall have performed the duty which I owe to my honour. The orders will not reach them until after my return, if I should return free, and consequently they will not have been unsealed. I shall take them back again. If I am delayed, it will be because some misfortune will have befallen me; and in that case assistance will be sent for me as well as for the King."

Prepared in this manner, the Superintendent arrived at the Bastille; he had travelled at the rate of five leagues and a half the hour. Every circumstance of delay which Aramis had escaped in his visit to the Bastille befell Fouquet. It was useless his giving his name, equally useless his being recognised: he could not succeed in obtaining an entrance. By dint of entreaties, threats, commands, he succeeded in inducing a sentinel to speak to one of the subalterns, who went and told the major. As for the governor, they did not even dare to disturb him. Fouquet sat in his carriage, at the outer gate of the fortress, chafing with rage and impatience, awaiting the return of the officers, who at last reappeared with a sufficiently sulky air.

"Well," said Fouquet impatiently, "what did the major say?"

"Well, monsieur," replied the soldier, "the major laughed in my face. He told me that M. Fouquet was at Vaux, and that even were he at Paris, M. Fouquet would not get up at so early an hour as the present."

"*Mordioux* ! you are a perfect set of fools," cried the minister, darting out of the carriage; and before the subaltern had had time to shut the gate Fouquet sprang through it, and ran forward in spite of the soldier, who cried out for assistance. Fouquet gained ground, regardless of the cries of the man, who, however, having at last come up with Fouquet, called out to the sentinel of the second gate. "Look out, look out, sentinel!" The man crossed his pike before the minister; but the latter, robust and active, and hurried away, too, by his passion, wrested the pike from the soldier, and struck him a violent blow on the shoulder with it. The subaltern, who approached too closely, received his part of the blows as well. Both of them uttered loud and furious cries, at the sound of which the whole of the first body of the advanced guard poured out of the guard-house. Among them there was one, however, who recognised the Superintendent, and who called out, "Monseigneur, ah, monseigneur! Stop, stop, you fellows!" And he effectually checked the soldiers, who were on the point of revenging their companions. Fouquet desired them to open the gate; but they refused to do so without the countersign; he desired them to inform the governor of his presence; but the latter had already heard the disturbance at the gate. He ran forward, followed by his major, and accompanied by a picket of twenty men, persuaded that an attack was being made on the Bastille. Baisemeaux also recognised Fouquet immediately, and dropped his sword, which he had held brandishing about in his hand.

"Ah! monseigneur," he stammered, "how can I excuse—"

"Monsieur," said the Superintendant, flushed with anger and heated by his exertions, "I congratulate you. Your watch and ward are admirably kept."

Baisemeaux turned pale, thinking that this remark was said ironically, and portended a furious burst of anger. But Fouquet had recovered his breath, and, beckoning towards him the sentinel and the subaltern, who were rubbing their shoulders, he said, "There are twenty pistoles for the sentinel, and fifty for the officer. Pray, receive my compliments, gentlemen. I will not fail to speak to His Majesty about you. And now, Monsieur Baisemeaux, a word with you."

And he followed the governor to his official residence, accompanied by a murmur of general satisfaction. Baisemeaux was already trembling with shame and uneasiness. Aramis's early visit, from that moment, seemed to possess consequences, which a functionary such as he (Baisemeaux) was, was perfectly justified in apprehending. It was quite another thing, however, when Fouquet, in a sharp tone of voice, and with an imperious look, said, "You have seen M. d'Herblay this morning?"

"Yes, monseigneur."

"And are you not horrified at the crime of which you have made yourself an accomplice?"

"Well," thought Baisemeaux, "good so far;" and then he

added, aloud, "But what crime, monseigneur, do you allude to?"

"That for which you can be quartered alive, monsieur,—do not forget that! But this is not a time to show anger. Conduct me immediately to the prisoner."

"To what prisoner?" said Baisemeaux tremblingly.

"You pretend to be ignorant? Very good—it is the best thing for you, perhaps, to do; for if, in fact, you were to admit your participation in it, it would be all over with you. I wish, therefore, to seem to believe in your assumption of ignorance."

"I entreat you, monseigneur—"

"That will do. Lead me to the prisoner."

"To Marchiali?"

"Who is Marchiali?"

"The prisoner who was brought back this morning by M. d'Herblay."

"He is called Marchiali?" said the Superintendant, his conviction somewhat shaken by Baisemeaux's cool manner.

"Yes, monseigneur; that is the name under which he was inscribed here."

Fouquet looked steadily at Baisemeaux, as if he would read his very heart; and perceived, with that clearsightedness which men possess who are accustomed to the exercise of power, that the man was speaking with the most perfect sincerity. Besides, in observing his face for a few moments, he could not believe that Aramis would have chosen such a confidant.

"It is the prisoner," said the Superintendant to him, "whom M. d'Herblay carried away the day before yesterday?"

"Yes, monseigneur."

"And whom he brought back this morning?" added Fouquet quickly: for he understood immediately the mechanism of Aramis's plan.

"Precisely, monseigneur."

"And his name is Marchiali, you say?"

"Yes, Marchiali. If monseigneur has come here to remove him, so much the better, for I was going to write about him."

"What has he done, then?"

"Ever since this morning he has annoyed me extremely. He has had such terrible fits of passion, as almost to make me believe that he would bring the Bastille itself down about our ears."

"I will soon relieve you of his presence," said Fouquet.

"Ah! so much the better."

"Conduct me to his prison."

"Will monseigneur give me the order?"

"What order?"

"An order from the King."

"Wait until I sign you one."

"That will not be sufficient, monseigneur. I must have an order from the King."

Fouquet assumed an irritated expression. "As you are so scrupulous," he said, "with regard to allowing prisoners to leave, show me the order by which this one was set at liberty."

Baisemeaux showed him the order to release Seldon.

"Very good," said Fouquet; "but Seldon is not Marchiali."

"But Marchiali is not at liberty, monseigneur; he is here."

"But you said that M. d'Herblay carried him away and brought him back again."

"I did not say so."

"So surely did you say it, that I almost seem to hear it now."

"It was a slip of my tongue, then, monseigneur."

"Take care, Monsieur Baisemeaux, take care."

"I have nothing to fear, monseigneur; I am acting according to strict regulation."

"Do you dare to say so?"

"I would say so in the presence of an apostle himself. M. d'Herblay brought me an order to set Seldon at liberty; and Seldon is free."

"I tell you that Marchiali has left the Bastille."

"You must prove that, monseigneur."

"Let me see him."

"You, monseigneur, who govern this kingdom, know very well that no one can see any of the prisoners without an express order from the King."

"M. d'Herblay has entered, however."

"That is to be proved, monseigneur."

"Monsieur de Baisemeaux, once more I warn you to pay particular attention to what you are saying."

"All the documents are there, monseigneur."

"M. d'Herblay is overthrown."

"Overthrown?—M. d'Herblay! Impossible!"

"You see that he has undoubtedly influenced you."

"No, monseigneur; what does, in fact, influence me, is the King's service. I am doing my duty. Give me an order from him, and you shall enter."

"Stay, monsieur, I give you my word that if you allow me to see the prisoner, I will give you an order from the King at once."

"Give me it now, monseigneur."

"And that, if you refuse me, I will have you and all your officers arrested on the spot."

"Before you commit such an act of violence, monseigneur, you will reflect," said Baisemeaux, who had turned very pale, "that we will only obey an order signed by the King; and that it will be just as easy for you to obtain one to see Marchiali as to obtain one to do me so much injury; me, too, who am perfectly innocent."

"True, true!" cried Fouquet furiously; "perfectly true, M. de Baisemeaux," he added, in a sonorous voice, drawing the unhappy governor towards him. "Do you know why I am so anxious to speak to the prisoner?"

"No, monseigneur; and allow me to observe that you are terrifying me out of my senses; I am trembling all over, and feel as if I were going to faint."

"You will stand a better chance of fainting outright, Monsieur Baisemeaux, when I return here at the head of ten thousand men and thirty pieces of cannon."

"Good Heavens, monseigneur, you are losing your senses."

"When I have raised the whole population of Paris against you and your cursed towers, and have battered open the gates of this place, and hanged you up to the bars of that tower in the corner there."

"Monseigneur! monseigneur! for pity's sake."

"I give you ten minutes to make up your mind," added Fouquet, in a calm voice. "I will sit down here, in this armchair, and wait for you; if, in ten minutes, time you still persist, I leave this place, and you may think me as mad as you like, but you will see."

Baisemeaux stamped his foot on the ground like a man in a state of despair, but he did not reply a single syllable; whereupon Fouquet seized a pen and ink, and wrote:—

"Order for M. le Prévôt des Marchands to assemble the municipal guard and to march upon the Bastille for the King's service."

Baisemeaux shrugged his shoulders. Fouquet wrote:—

"Order for the Duc de Bouillon and M. le Prince de Condé to assume command of the Swiss guards, of the King's guards, and to march upon the Bastille for the King's service."

Baisemeaux reflected. Fouquet still wrote:—

"Order for every soldier, citizen, or gentleman to seize and apprehend, wherever he may be found, the Chevalier d'Herblay, Bishop of Vannes, and his accomplices, who are: Ist, M. de Baisemeaux, governor of the Bastille, suspected of the crimes of high treason and rebellion—"

"Stop, monseigneur!" cried Baisemeaux; "I do not understand a single thing of the whole matter; but so many misfortunes, even were it madness itself that had set them at work, might happen here in a couple of hours, that the

King, by whom I shall be judged, will see whether I have been wrong in withdrawing the countersign before so many imminent catastrophes. Come with me to the keep, monseigneur; you shall see Marchiali."

Fouquet darted out of the room, followed by Baisemeaux as he wiped the perspiration from his face. "What a terrible morning!" he said. "What a disgrace!"

"Walk faster," replied Fouquet.

Baisemeaux made a sign to the jailer to precede them. He was afraid of his companion, which the latter could not fail to perceive.

"A truce to this child's play," he said roughly. "Let the man remain here, take the keys yourself, and show me the way. Not a single person, do you understand, must hear what is going to take place here."

"Ah!" said Baisemeaux, undecided.

"Again, 'Ah!' "cried Fouquet. "Say 'no' at once, and I will leave the Bastille and will myself carry my own dispatches."

Baisemeaux bowed his head, took the keys, and unaccompanied, except by the minister, ascended the staircase. The higher they advanced up the spiral staircase, certain smothered murmurs became distinct cries and fearful imprecations. "What is that?" asked Fouquet.

"That is your Marchiali," said the governor; "that is the way these madmen call out."

And he accompanied that reply with a glance more indicative of injurious allusions, as far as Fouquet was concerned, than of politeness. The latter trembled; he had just recognised in one cry more terrible than any that had preceded it, the King's voice. He paused on the staircase, snatching the bunch of keys from Baisemeaux, who thought this new madman was going to dash out his brains with one of them. "Ah!" he cried, "M. d'Herblay did not say a word about that."

"Give me the keys at once!" cried Fouquet, tearing them from his hand. "Which is the key of the door I am to open?"

"That one."

A fearful cry, followed by a violent blow against the door, made the whole staircase resound with the echo. "Leave this place," said Fouquet to Baisemeaux, in a threatening voice.

"I ask nothing better," murmured the latter. "There will be a couple of madmen face to face, and the one will kill the other, I am sure."

"Go!" repeated Fouquet. "If you place your foot on this staircase before I call you, remember that you shall take the place of the meanest prisoner in the Bastille."

"This job will kill me, I am sure it will," muttered Baisemeaux, as he withdrew with tottering steps.

The prisoner's cries became more and more terrible. When Fouquet had satisfied himself that Baisemeaux had reached the bottom of the staircase, he inserted the key in the first lock. It was then that he heard the hoarse, choking voice of the King, crying out, in a frenzy of rage, "Help, help ! I am the King." The key of the second door was not the same as the first, and Fouquet was obliged to look for it on the bunch. The King, however, furious and almost mad with rage and passion, shouted at the top of his voice, "It was M. Fouquet who brought me here. Help me against M. Fouquet! I am the King! Help the King against M. Fouquet!"

These cries tore the minister's heart with mingled emotions. They were followed by a shower of terrible blows levelled against the door with a part of the broken chair with which the King had armed himself. Fouquet at last succeeded in finding the key. The King was almost exhausted; he could hardly articulate distinctly as he shouted, "Death to Fouquet! Death to the traitor Fouquet!"

The door flew open.

15

The King's Gratitude

The two men were on the point of darting towards each other when they suddenly and abruptly stopped, as a mutual recognition took place, and each uttered a cry of horror.

"Have you come to assassinate me, monsieur?" said the King, when he recognised Fouquet.

"The King in this state!" murmured the minister.

Nothing could be more terrible indeed than the appearance of the young Prince at the moment Fouquet had surprised him; his clothes were in tatters; his shirt, open and torn to rags, was stained with sweat and with the blood which streamed from his lacerated breast and arms. Haggard, ghastly pale, his hair in dishevelled masses, Louis XIV presented the most perfect picture of despair, hunger, and fear combined, that could possibly be united in one figure. Fouquet was so touched, so affected and disturbed by it, that he ran towards him with his arms stretched out and his eyes filled with tears. Louis held up the massive piece of wood of which he had made such a furious use.

"Sire," said Fouquet, in a voice trembling with emotion, "do you not recognise the most faithful of your friends?"

"A friend—you!" repeated Louis, gnashing his teeth in a manner which betrayed his hate and desire for speedy vengeance.

"The most respectful of your servants," added Fouquet, throwing himself on his knees. The King let the rude weapon fall from his grasp. Fouquet approached him, kissed his knees, and took him in his arms with inconceivable tenderness.

"My King, my child," he said, "how you must have suffered!"

Louis recalled to himself by the change of situation, looked at himself, and ashamed of the disordered state of his apparel, ashamed of his conduct, and ashamed of the air of pity and protection that was shown towards him, drew back. Fouquet did not understand this movement; he did not perceive that the King's feeling of pride would never forgive him for having been a witness of such an exhibition of weakness.

"Come, sire," he said, "you are free."

"Free?" repeated the King. "Oh, you set me at liberty, then, after having dared to lift up your hand against me."

"You do not believe that!" exclaimed Fouquet indignantly. "You cannot believe me to be guilty of such an act."

And rapidly, warmly even, he related the whole particulars of the intrigue, the details of which are already known to the reader. While the recital continued, Louis suffered the most horrible anguish of mind; and when it was finished, the magnitude of the danger he had run struck him far more than the importance of the secret relative to his twin brother.

"Monsieur," he said suddenly to Fouquet, "this double birth is a falsehood; it is impossible—you cannot have been the dupe of it."

"Sire!"

"It is impossible, I tell you, that the honour, the virtue of my mother can be suspected. And my first minister has not yet done justice on the criminals?"

"Reflect, sire, before you are hurried away by your anger," replied Fouquet. "The birth of your brother—"

"I have only one brother—and that is *Monsieur*. You know it as well as myself. There is a plot, I tell you, beginning with the governor of the Bastille."

"Be careful, sire, for this man has been deceived as every one else has by the Prince's likeness to yourself."

"Likeness! Absurd!"

"This Marchiali must be singularly like your Majesty to be able to deceive every one's eye," Fouquet persisted.

"Ridiculous."

"Do not say so, sire; those who had prepared everything in order to face and deceive your ministers, your mother, your officers of state, the members of your family, must be quite confident of the resemblance between you."

"But where are these persons, then?" murmured the King.

"At Vaux."

"At Vaux! And you suffer them to remain there!"

"My most pressing duty seemed to be your Majesty's release. I have accomplished that duty; and now, whatever your Majesty may command, shall be done. I await your orders."

Louis reflected for a few moments.

"Muster all the troops in Paris," he said.

"All the necessary orders are given for that purpose," replied Fouquet.

"You have given orders!" exclaimed the King.

"For that purpose, yes, sire; your Majesty will be at the head of ten thousand men in less than an hour."

The only reply the King made was to take hold of Fouquet's hand with such an expression of feeling, that it was very easy to perceive how strongly he had, until that remark, maintained his suspicions of the minister, notwithstanding the latter's intervention.

"And with these troops," he said, "we shall go at once and besiege in your house the rebels who by this time will have established and entrenched themselves there."

"I should be surprised if that were the case," replied Fouquet.

"Why?"

"Because their chief—the very soul of the enterprise—having been unmasked by me, the whole plan seems to me to have miscarried."

"You have unmasked this false prince also?"

"No, I have not seen him."

"Whom have you seen, then?"

"The leader of the enterprise, not that unhappy young man; the latter is merely an instrument, destined through his whole life to wretchedness, I plainly perceive."

"Most certainly."

"It is M. l'Abbé d'Herblay, Bishop of Vannes."

"Your friend."

"He was my friend, sire," replied Fouquet nobly.

"An unfortunate circumstance for you," said the King, in a less generous tone of voice.

"Such friendships, sire, had nothing dishonourable in them so long as I was ignorant of the crime."

"You should have foreseen it."

"If I am guilty, I place myself in your Majesty's hands."

"Ah, Monsieur Fouquet, it was not that I meant," returned the King, sorry to have shown the bitterness of his thoughts in such a manner. "Well! I assure you that notwithstanding the mask with which the villain covered his face, I had something like a vague suspicion that it might be he. But with this chief of the enterprise there was a man of prodigious strength, the one who menaced me with a force almost herculean; what is he?"

"It must be his friend the Baron du Vallon, Porthos, formerly one of the musketeers."

"The friend of d'Artagnan? the friend of the Comte de la Fère. Ah!" exclaimed the King, as he paused at the name of the latter, "we must not forget the connection that existed between the conspirators and M. de Bragelonne."

"Sire, sire, do not go too far! M. de la Fère is the most honourable man in France. Be satisfied with those whom I deliver up to you."

"With those whom you deliver up to me, you say? Very good, for you will deliver up those who are guilty to me."

"What does your Majesty understand by that?" inquired Fouquet.

"I understand," replied the King, "that we shall soon arrive at Vaux with a large body of troops, that we will lay violent hands upon that nest of vipers, and that not a soul shall escape."

"Your Majesty will put these men to death?" cried Fouquet.

"To the very meanest of them."

"Oh, sire!"

"Let us understand each other, Monsieur Fouquet," said the King haughtily. "We no longer live in times when assassination was the only and the last resource which kings had in their power. No! Heaven be praised! I have Parliaments who sit and judge in my name, and I have scaffolds on which my supreme authority is carried out."

Fouquet turned pale. "I will take the liberty of observing to your Majesty, that any proceedings instituted respecting these matters would bring down the greatest scandal upon the dignity of the throne. The august name of Anne of Austria must never be allowed to pass the lips of the people accompanied by a smile."

"Justice must be done, however, monsieur."

"Good, sire; but the royal blood cannot be shed on a scaffold."

"The royal blood! You believe that!" cried the King, with fury in his voice, stamping his foot on the ground. "This double birth is an invention; and in that invention particularly, do I see M. d'Herblay's crime. It is the crime I wish to punish rather than their violence, or their insult."

"And punish it with death, sire?"

"With death; yes, monsieur."

"Sire," said the Superintendant with firmness, as he raised his head proudly, "your Majesty will take the life, if you please, of your brother Philippe of France; that concerns you alone, and you will doubtless consult the Queen-Mother upon the subject. Whatever she may command will be perfectly correct. I do not wish to mix myself up in it, not even for the honour of your crown, but I have a favour to ask of you, and I beg to submit it to you."

"Speak," said the King, in no little degree agitated by his minister's last words. "What do you require?"

"The pardon of M. d'Herblay and M. du Vallon."

"My assassins?"

"Two rebels, sire, that is all."

"Oh, I understand, then, you ask me to forgive your friends."

"My friends!" said Fouquet, deeply wounded.

"Your friends, certainly; but the safety of the State requires that an exemplary punishment should be inflicted on the guilty."

"I will not permit myself to remind your Majesty that I have just restored you to liberty, and have saved your life."

"Monsieur!"

"I will not allow myself to remind your Majesty that had M. d'Herblay wished to carry out his character of assassin, he could very easily have assassinated your Majesty this morning in the forest of Sénart, and all would have been over."

The King started.

"A pistol bullet through the head," pursued Fouquet, "and the disfigured features of Louis XIV, which no one could have recognised, would be M. d'Herblay's complete and entire justification."

The King turned pale and giddy at the idea of the danger he had escaped.

"If M. d'Herblay,' continued Fouquet, "had been an assassin, he had no occasion to inform me of his plan, in order to succeed. Freed from the real king, it would have been impossible to guess the false king. And if the usurper had been recognised by Anne of Austria, he would have still been a son for her. The usurper, as far as Monsieur d'Herblay's conscience was concerned, was still a king of the blood of Louis XIII. Moreover, the conspirator, in that course, would have had security, secrecy, and impunity. A pistol-bullet would have procured him all that. For the sake of Heaven, sire, grant me his forgiveness."

The King, instead of being touched by the picture he had drawn, so faithful in all its details, of Aramis's generosity, felt himself most painfully and cruelly humiliated by it. His unconquerable pride revolted at the idea that a man had held suspended at the end of his finger the thread of his royal life. Every word that fell from Fouquet's lips, and which he thought most efficacious in procuring his friend's pardon, seemed to pour another drop of poison into the already ulcerated heart of Louis XIV. Nothing could bend or soften him. Addressing himself to Fouquet, he said, "I really don't know, monsieur, why you should solicit the pardon of these men. What good is there in asking that which can be obtained without solicitation?"

"I do not understand you, sire."

"It is not difficult, either. Where am I now?"

"In the Bastille, sire."

"Yes; in a dungeon. I am looked upon as a madman, am I not?"

"Yes, sire."

"And no one is known here but Marchiali?"

"Certainly."

"Well; change nothing in the position of affairs. Let the madman rot in the dungeon of the Bastille, and M. d'Herblay and M. du Vallon will stand in no need of my forgiveness. Their new king will absolve them."

"Your Majesty does me a great injustice, sire; and you are wrong," replied Fouquet dryly; "I am not child enough, nor is M. d'Herblay silly enough to have omitted to make all these reflections; and if I had wished to make a new king, as you say, I had no occasion to have come here to force open all the gates and doors of the Bastille, to free you from this place. That would show a want of common sense even. Your Majesty's mind is disturbed by anger; otherwise you would be far from offending, groundlessly, the very one of your servants who has rendered you the most important service of all."

Louis perceived that he had gone too far, that the gates of the Bastille were still closed upon him; whilst, by degrees, the floodgates were gradually being opened behind which the generous-hearted Fouquet had restrained his anger. "I did not say that to humiliate you, Heaven knows, monsieur," he replied. "Only you are addressing yourself to me, in order to obtain a pardon, and I answer you according as my conscience dictates. And so, judging by my conscience, the criminals we speak of are not worthy of consideration or forgiveness."

Fouquet was silent.

"What I do is as generous," added the King, "as what you have done, for I am in your power. I will even say, it is more generous, inasmuch as you place before me certain conditions, upon which my liberty, my life, may depend; and to reject which is to make a sacrifice of them both."

"I was wrong, certainly," replied Fouquet. "Yes—I had the appearance of extorting a favour; I regret it, and entreat your Majesty's forgiveness."

"And you are forgiven, my dear Monsieur Fouquet," said the King, with a smile, which restored the serene expression of his features which so many circumstances had altered since the preceding evening.

"I have my own forgiveness," replied the minister, with some degree of persistence; "but M. d'Herblay, and M. du Vallon?"

"They will never obtain theirs as long as I live," replied the inflexible King. "Do me the kindness not to speak of it again."

"Your Majesty shall be obeyed."

"And you will bear me no ill will for it?"

"Oh, no, sire; for I anticipated it as being most likely."

"You had 'anticipated' that I should refuse to forgive those gentlemen?"

"Certainly; and all my measures were taken in consequence."

"What do you mean to say?" cried the King, surprised.

"M. d'Herblay came, as may be said, to deliver himself into my hands. M. d'Herblay left to me the happiness of saving my King and my country. I could not condemn M. d'Herblay to death; nor could I, on the other hand, expose him to your Majesty's most justifiable wrath; it would have been just the same as if I had killed him myself."

"Well; and what have you done?"

"Sire, I gave M. d'Herblay the best horses in my stables, and four hours' start over all those your Majesty might, probably, dispatch after him."

"Be it so!" murmured the King. "But still, the world is wide enough and large enough for those whom I may send to overtake your horses, notwithstanding the 'four hours' start' which you have given to M. d'Herblay."

"In giving him those four hours, sire, I knew I was giving him his life, and he will save his life."

"In what way?"

"After having galloped as hard as possible, with the four hours' start, before your musketeers, he will reach my château of Belle-Isle, where I have given him a safe asylum."

"That may be! But you forget that you have made me a present of Belle-Isle."

"But not for you to arrest my friends."

"You take it back again, then?"

"As far as that goes—yes, sire."

"My musketeers will capture it, and the affair will be at an end."

"Neither your musketeers, nor your whole army could take Belle-Isle," said Fouquet coldly. "Belle-Isle is impregnable."

The King became perfectly livid; a lightning flash seemed to dart from his eyes. Fouquet felt that he was lost, but he was not one to shrink when the voice of honour spoke loudly within him. He bore the King's wrathful gaze; the latter swallowed his rage, and after a few moments' silence, said, "When we return, you will consider yourself under arrest!"

"I am at your Majesty's orders," replied Fouquet, with a low bow.

"Come," said the King. And they left the prison, passing before Baisemeaux, who looked completely bewildered as he saw Marchiali once more leave; and, in his helplessness, tore out the few remaining hairs he had left. It was perfectly true, however, that Fouquet wrote and gave him an authority for the prisoner's release, and that the King wrote beneath it, "Seen and approved, Louis"; a piece of madness that Baisemeaux, incapable of putting two ideas together, acknowledged by giving himself a terrible blow with his fist on his jaws.

16

The False King

In the meantime, usurped royalty was playing out its part bravely at Vaux. Philippe gave orders for a full reception at his *petit lever*. He determined to give this order notwithstanding the absence of M. d'Herblay, who did not return, and our readers know for what reason. But the Prince, not believing that absence could be prolonged, wished, as all rash spirits do, to try his valour and his fortune when far from all protection and all counsel. Another reason urged him to do this: Anne of Austria was about to appear; the guilty mother was about to stand in the presence of her sacrificed son. Philippe was not willing, if he had a weakness, to render the man a witness of it, before whom he was bound thenceforth to display so much strength. Philippe opened his folding doors, and several persons entered silently. Philippe did not stir whilst his *valets-de-chambre* dressed him. He had watched, the evening before, all the habits of his brother, and played the king in such a manner as to awaken no suspicion. He was then completely dressed in his hunting costume, when he received his visitors. His own memory and the notes of Aramis announced everybody to him, first of all the Queen-Mother, Anne of Austria, to whom Monsieur, her younger son, gave his hand, and then his wife, Henrietta, with M. de Saint-Aignan, the King's favourite. He smiled at seeing these countenances, but trembled on recognising his mother. That figure so noble, so imposing, ravaged by pain, pleaded in his heart the cause of that famous Queen who had immolated a child to reasons of State.

He found his mother still handsome. He knew that Louis XIV loved her, and he promised himself to love her likewise, and not to prove a cruel chastisement for her old age. He contemplated his brother with a tenderness easily to be understood. The latter had usurped nothing over him, had cast no shade over his life. A separate branch, he allowed the stem to rise without heeding its elevation or the majesty of its life. Philippe promised himself to be a kind brother to this Prince, who required nothing but gold to minister to his pleasures. He bowed with a friendly air to Saint-Aignan, who was all reverences and smiles, and tremblingly held out his hand to Henrietta, his sister-in-law, whose beauty struck him; but he saw in the eyes of that Princess an expression of coldness which would facilitate, as he thought, their future relations.

"How much more easy," thought he, "it will be to be the brother of that woman than her gallant, if she evinces towards me a coldness that my brother could not have for her, and which is imposed upon me as a duty." The only visit he dreaded at this moment was that of the Queen; his heart—his mind—had just been shaken by so violent a trial, that, in spite of their firm temperament, they would not, perhaps, support another shock. Happily the Queen did not come. Then commenced, on the part of Anne of Austria, a political dissertation upon the welcome M. Fouquet had given to the house of France. She mixed up hostilities with compliments addressed to the King and questions as to his health, with little maternal flatteries and diplomatic artifices.

"Well, my son," said she, "are you convinced with regard to M. Fouquet?"

"Saint-Aignan," said Philippe, "have the goodness to go and inquire after the Queen."

At these words, the first Philippe had pronounced aloud, the slight difference that there was between his voice and that of the King was sensible to maternal ears, and Anne of

Austria looked earnestly at her son. Saint-Aignan left the room, and Philippe continued. "Madame, I do not like to hear M. Fouquet ill-spoken of, you know I do not—and you have even spoken well of him yourself."

"That is true; therefore I only question you on the state of your sentiments with respect to him."

"Sire," said Henrietta, "I, on my part, have always liked M. Fouquet. He is a man of good taste—he is a superior man."

"A Superintendant who is never sordid or niggardly," added Monsieur; "and who pays in gold all the orders I have on him."

"Every one in this thinks too much of himself, and nobody for the State," said the old Queen. "M. Fouquet, it is a fact, M. Fouquet is ruining the State."

"Well, mother!" replied Philippe, in rather a lower key, "do you likewise constitute yourself the buckler of M. Colbert?"

"You know all, sire," said the Queen, more uneasy than irritated.

Her son had pity on her. He took her hand and kissed it tenderly; she did not feel that in that kiss, given in spite of repulsions and bitternesses of the heart, there was a pardon for six years of horrible suffering. Philippe allowed the silence of a moment to swallow the emotions that had just developed themselves. Then, with a cheerful smile:—

"We will not go today," said he, "I have a plan." And, turning towards the door, he hoped to see Aramis, whose absence began to alarm him. The Queen-Mother wished to leave the room.

"Remain where you are, mother," said he, "I wish you to make your peace with M. Fouquet."

"I bear no ill towards M. Fouquet; I only dreaded his prodigalities."

"We will put that to rights, and will take nothing of the Superintendant but his good qualities."

"What is your Majesty looking for?" said Henrietta, seeing the King's eyes constantly turned towards the door, and wishing to let fly a little poisoned arrow at his heart, supposing he was so anxiously expecting either La Vallière or a letter from her.

"My sister," said the young man, who had divined her thought, thanks to that marvellous perspicuity of which fortune was from that time about to allow him the exercise, "my sister, I am expecting a most distinguished man, a most able counsellor, whom I wish to present to you all, recommending him to your good graces. Ah, come in then, d'Artagnan."

"What does your Majesty wish?" said d'Artagnan, appearing.

"Where is monsieur the Bishop of Vannes, your friend?"

"Why, sire—"

"I am waiting for him, and he does not come. Let him be sought for."

D'Artagnan remained for an instant stupefied; but soon, reflecting that Aramis had left Vaux secretly with a mission from the King, he concluded that the King wished to preserve the secret of it. "Sire," replied he, "does your Majesty absolutely require M. d'Herblay to be brought to you?"

"Absolutely is not the word," said Philippe; "I do not want him so particularly as that; but if he can be found—"

"I thought so," said d'Artagnan to himself.

"Is this M. d'Herblay Bishop of Vannes?"

"Yes, madame."

"A friend of M. Fouquet?"

"Yes, madame, an old musketeer."

Anne of Austria blushed.

"One of the four braves who formerly performed such wonders."

The old Queen repented of having wished to bite; she broke off the conversation, in order to preserve the rest of her teeth. "Whatever may be your choice, sire," said she, "I have no doubt it will be excellent."

All bowed in support of that sentiment.

"You will find in him," continued Philippe, "the depth and penetration of M. de Richelieu, without the avarice of M. de Mazarin."

"A prime minister, sire?" said Monsieur in a fright.

"I will tell you all about that, brother; but it is strange that M. d'Herblay is not here!" He called out:—

"Let M. Fouquet be informed that I wish to speak to him."

M. de Saint-Aignan returned, bringing satisfactory news of the Queen, who only kept her bed from precaution, and to have strength to carry out all the King's wishes. Whilst everybody was seeking M. Fouquet and Aramis, the new King quietly continued his experiments, and everybody, family, officers, servants, had not the least suspicion, his air, voice, and manners, were so like the King's. On his side, Philippe, applying to all countenances the faithful notice and design furnished by his accomplice Aramis, conducted himself so as not to give birth to a doubt in the minds of those who surrounded him. Nothing from that time could disturb the usurper. With what strange facility had Providence just reversed the most elevated fortune of the world to substitute the most humble in his stead! Philippe admired the goodness of God with regard to himself, and seconded it with all the resources of his admirable nature. But he felt, at times, something like a shadow gliding between him and the rays of his new glory. Aramis did not appear. The conversation had languished in the royal family; Philippe, preoccupied, forgot to dismiss his brother and Madame Henrietta. The latter were astonished, and began, by degrees, to lose all patience. Anne of Austria stooped towards her son's ear, and addressed some words to him in Spanish. Philippe was completely ignorant of that language; and grew pale at this unexpected obstacle. But, as if the spirit of the imperturbable Aramis had covered him with his infallibility, instead of appearing disconcerted, Phillipe rose. "Well, what?" said Anne of Austria.

"What is all that noise?" said Philippe, turning round towards the door of the second staircase.

And a voice was heard, saying: "This way! This way! A few steps more, sire!"

"The voice of M. Fouquet," said d'Artagnan, who was standing close to the Queen-Mother.

"Then M. d'Herblay cannot be far off," added Philippe.

But he then saw what he little thought to see so near to him. All eyes were turned towards the door at which M. Fouquet was expected to enter; but it was not M. Fouquet who entered. A terrible cry resounded from all corners of the chamber, a painful cry uttered by the King and all present. It is not given to men, even to those whose destiny contains the strangest elements, and accidents the most wonderful, to contemplate a spectacle similar to that which presented itself in the royal chamber at that moment. The half-closed shutters only admitted the entrance of an uncertain light passing through large velvet curtains lined with silk. In this soft shade, the eyes were by degrees dilated, and every one present saw others rather with trust than with positive sight. There could not, however, escape, in these circumstances, one of the surrounding details; and the new object which presented itself appeared as luminous as if it had been enlightened by the sun. So it happened with Louis XIV, when he showed himself pale and frowning in the doorway of the secret stairs. The face of Fouquet appeared behind him, impressed with sorrow and sternness. The Queen-Mother, who perceived Louis XIV, and who held the hand of Philippe, uttered the cry of which we have spoken, as if she had beheld a phantom. Monsieur was bewildered, and kept turning his head in astonishment from one to the other. Henrietta made a step forward, thinking she saw the form of her brother-in-law reflected in a glass. And, in fact, the illusion was possible. The two princes, both pale as death—for we renounce the hope of being able to describe the fearful state of Philippe—both trembling, and clenching their hands convulsively, measured each other with their looks, and darted their eyes like poniards, into each other. Mute, panting, bending forward, they appeared as if about to spring upon an enemy. The unheard of resemblance of countenance, gesture, shape, height, even to the resemblance of costume, produced by chance—for Louis XIV had been to the Louvre and put on a violet-coloured dress—the perfect analogy of the two princes, completed the consternation of Anne of Austria. And yet she did not at once guess the truth. There are misfortunes in life that no one will accept; people would rather believe in the supernatural and the impossible. Louis had not reckoned upon these obstacles. He expected he had only to appear and be acknowledged. A living sun, he could not endure the suspicion of parity with any one. He did not admit that every torch should not become darkness at the instant he shone out with his conquering ray. At the aspect of Philippe, then, he was, perhaps, more terrified than any one round him, and his silence, his immobility were, this time, a concentration and a calm which precede violent explosions of passion.

But Fouquet! Who could paint his emotion and stupor in presence of this living portrait of his master? Fouquet thought Aramis was right, that this newly arrived was a king as pure in his race as the other, and that, for having repudiated all participation in this *coup d'état*, so skilfully got up by the General of the Jesuits, he must be a mad enthusiast unworthy of ever again dipping his hands in a political work. And then it was the blood of Louis XIII which Fouquet was sacrificing to the blood of Louis XIII; it was to a selfish ambition he was sacrificing a noble ambition; it was to the right of keeping he sacrificed the right of having. The whole extent of his fault was revealed to him by the simple sight of the pretender. All which passed in the mind of Fouquet was lost upon the persons present. He had five minutes to concentrate his meditations upon this point of the case of conscience; five minutes, that is to say five ages, during which the two kings and their family scarcely found time to breathe after so terrible a shock. D'Artagnan, leaning against the wall, in front of Fouquet, with his hand to his brow, asked himself the cause of such a wonderful prodigy. He could not have said at once why he doubted, but he knew assuredly that he had reason to doubt, and that in this meeting of the two Louis XIVs lay all the difficulty which during late days had rendered the conduct of Aramis so suspicious to the musketeer. These ideas were, however, enveloped in thick veils. The actors in this assembly seemed to swim in the vapours of a confused waking. Suddenly Louis XIV, more impatient and more accustomed to command, ran to one of the shutters, which he opened, tearing the curtains in his eagerness. A flood of living light entered the chamber, and made Philippe draw back to the alcove. Louis seized upon this movement with eagerness, and addressing himself to the Queen-Mother,—

"My mother," said he, "do you not acknowledge your son, since every one here has forgotten his King!" Anne of Austria started, and raised her arms towards Heaven, without being able to articulate a single word.

"My mother," said Philippe, with a calm voice, "do you not acknowledge your son?" And this time, in his turn, Louis drew back.

As to Anne of Austria, struck in both head and heart with remorse, she lost her equilibrium. No one aiding her, for all were petrified, she sank back in her chair, breathing a weak, trembling sigh. Louis could not endure this spectacle and this affront. He bounded towards d'Artagnan, upon whom the vertigo was beginning to gain, and who staggered as he caught at the door, for support.

"Captain," said he, "look us in the face and say which is the paler, he or I!"

This cry roused d'Artagnan, and stirred in his heart the fibre of obedience. He shook his head, and, without more hesitation, he walked straight up to Philippe, upon whose shoulder he laid his hand, saying, "Monsieur, you are my prisoner!"

Philippe did not raise his eyes towards Heaven, nor stir from the spot, where he seemed nailed to the floor, his eye intensely fixed upon the King his brother. He reproached him by a sublime silence with all his misfortunes past, with all his tortures to come. Against this language of the soul the King felt he had no power; he cast down his eyes, and passed quickly out of the door, forgetting his mother, sitting motionless within three paces of the son whom she left a second time to be condemned to death. Philippe approached Anne of Austria, and said to her, in a soft and nobly agitated voice,—

"If I were not your son, I should curse you, my mother, for having rendered me so unhappy."

D'Artagnan felt a shudder pass through the marrow of his bones. He bowed respectfully to the young Prince, and said, as he bent, "Excuse me, monseigneur, I am but a soldier, and my oaths are his who has just left the chamber."

"Thank you, M. d'Artagnan. But what is become of M. d'Herblay?"

"M. d'Herblay is in safety, monseigneur," said a voice behind them; "and no one, while I live and am free, shall cause a hair to fall from his head."

"Monsieur Fouquet!" said the Prince, smiling sadly.

"Pardon me, monseigneur," said Fouquet, kneeling, "but he who is just gone out from hence was my guest, though I am no longer his servant."

"Here are," murmured Philippe, with a sigh, "brave friends and good hearts. They make me regret the world. On, M. d'Artagnan, I follow you."

At the moment the captain of the musketeers was about to leave the room with his prisoner, Colbert appeared, and, after remitting an order from the King to d'Artagnan, retired. D'Artagnan read the paper, and then crushed it in his hand with rage.

"What is it?" asked the Prince.

"Read, monseigneur," replied the musketeer.

Philippe read the following words, hastily traced by the hand of the King:—"M. d'Artagnan will conduct the prisoner to the Ile Sainte-Marguerite. He will cover his face with an iron visor, which the prisoner cannot raise without peril of his life."

"That is just," said Philippe, with resignation, "I am ready."

"Aramis was right," said Fouquet, in a low voice to the musketeer; "this one is quite as much of a king as the other."

"More!" replied d'Artagnan. "He only wants you and me."

17

In Which Porthos Thinks He Is Pursuing A Duchy

Aramis and Porthos, having profited by the time granted them by Fouquet, did honour to the French cavalry by their speed. Porthos did not clearly understand for what kind of mission he was forced to display so much velocity; but as he saw Aramis spurring on furiously, he, Porthos, spurred on in the same manner. They had soon, in this manner, placed twelve leagues between them and Vaux; and stopping only to change horses at intervals, they rode on till they reached Blois at seven o'clock in the evening. Here Aramis proposed a visit to the Comte de la Fère who also lived in the neighbourhood. Porthos ventured to interrogate his companion discreetly.

"Hush!" replied the latter. "Know only that our fortune depends upon our speed."

"I shall be made a duke!" said Porthos aloud. He was speaking to himself.

"That is possible," replied Aramis, smiling after his own fashion, as the horse of Porthos passed him. The head of Aramis was, notwithstanding, on fire; the activity of the body had not yet succeeded in subduing that of the mind. All that there is in raging passions, in severe toothaches, or mortal threats, twisted, gnawed, and grumbled in the thoughts of the vanquished prelate.

"We are going, on the part of the King, to make some great proposal to Athos," suggested Porthos.

"Pooh!" said Aramis.

"You need tell me nothing about it," added the worthy Porthos, "I shall guess."

"Well, do, my friend; guess away."

They arrived at Athos's dwelling about nine o'clock in the evening, favoured by a splendid moon. This cheerful light rejoiced Porthos beyond expression; but Aramis appeared annoyed by it in an equal degree. He could not help showing something of this to Porthos, who replied, "Ay, ay! I guess how it is! The mission is a secret one."

The driver interrupted him by saying, "Gentlemen, you are arrived."

Porthos and his companion alighted before the gate of the little château. Athos and his son, Raoul were, as usual, conversing and walking backwards and forwards in the long alley of limes in the park, when the bell which served to announce to the Comte either the hour of dinner or the arrival of a visitor, was rung; and, without attaching any importance to it, he turned towards the house with his son; and at the end of the alley they found themselves in the presence of Aramis and Porthos.

Raoul uttered a cry, and affectionately embraced Porthos. Aramis and Athos embraced like old men; and this embrace itself being a question for Aramis, he immediately said, "My friend, we have not long to remain with you."

"Ah!" said the Comte.

"Only time to tell you of my good fortune," interrupted Porthos.

"Ah!" said Raoul.

Athos looked silently at Aramis, whose sombre air had already appeared to him very little in harmony with the good news Porthos spoke of.

"What is the good fortune that has happened to you? Let us hear it," said Raoul, with a smile.

"The King has made me a duke," said the worthy Porthos, with an air of mystery, in the ear of the young man, "a duke by brevet."

But the asides of Porthos were always loud enough to be heard by everybody. His murmurs were in the diapason of ordinary roaring. Athos heard him, and uttered an exclamation which made Aramis start. The latter took Athos by the arm, and, after having asked Porthos's permission to say a word to his friend in private, "My dear Athos," he began, "you see me overwhelmed with grief."

"With grief, my dear friend?" cried the Comte. "Oh, what?"

"In two words, I have raised a conspiracy against the King; that conspiracy has failed, and, at this moment, I am doubtless pursued."

"You are pursued!—A conspiracy, Eh! my friend, what do you tell me?"

"A sad truth. I am entirely ruined."

"Well, but Porthos—this title of duke—what does all that mean?"

"That is the subject of my severest pain; that is the deepest of my wounds. I have, believing in an infallible success, drawn Porthos into my conspiracy. He has thrown himself into it, as you know he would do, with all his strength, without knowing what he was about; and now, he is as much compromised as myself—as completely ruined as I am."

"Good God!" And Athos turned towards Porthos, who was smiling complacently.

"I must make you acquainted with the whole. Listen to me," continued Aramis; and he related the history as we know it. Athos, during the recital, several times felt the sweat break from his forehead. "It was a great idea," said he, "but a great error."

"For which I am punished, Athos."

"Therefore, I will not tell you my entire thought."

"Tell it, nevertheless."

"It is a crime."

"Capital. I know it is. *Lèse majesté*."

"Porthos, poor Porthos!"

"What would you advise me to do? Success as I have told you, was certain."

"M. Fouquet is an honest man."

"And I am a fool for having so ill judged of him," said Aramis, "Oh, the wisdom of man! Oh, vast millstone which grinds the world! and which is one day stopped by a grain of sand which has fallen, no one knows how, in its wheels."

"Say, by a diamond, Aramis. But the thing is done. How do you think of acting?"

"I am taking away Porthos. The King will never believe that that worthy man has acted innocently. He can never believe that Porthos has thought he was serving the King whilst acting as he has done. His head would pay for my fault. It shall not be so."

"You are taking him away; whither?"

"To Belle-Isle, at first. That is an impregnable place of refuge. Then I have the sea, and a vessel to pass over into England, where I have many relations."

"You? In England?"

"Yes, or else into Spain, where I have still more."

"But, our excellent Porthos—you ruin him, for the King will confiscate all his property."

"All is provided for. I know how, when once in Spain, to reconcile myself with Louis XIV, and restore Porthos to favour."

"You have credit, seemingly, Aramis," said Athos, with a discreet air.

"Much; and at the service of my friends."

These words were accompanied by a warm pressure of the hand.

"Thank you," replied the Comte.

"And while we are on that head," said Aramis, "you also are a malcontent. Follow our example; pass over into Belle-Isle. Then we shall see, I guarantee upon my honour, that in a month there will be war between France and Spain on the subject of this son of Louis XIII, who is an Infante likewise, and whom France detains inhumanly. Now, as Louis XIV would have no inclination for a war on that subject, I will answer for a transaction, the result of which must bring greatness to Porthos and to me, and a duchy in France to you, who are already a grandee of Spain. Will you join us?"

"No; for my part I prefer having something to reproach the King with; it is a pride natural to my race to pretend to a superiority over royal races. Doing what you propose, I should become the obliged of the King; I should certainly be a gainer on that ground, but I should be a loser in my conscience.—No, thank you!"

"Then, give me two things, Athos,—your absolution."

"Oh, I give it you if you have really wished to avenge the weak and the oppressed against the oppressor."

"That is sufficient for me," said Aramis, with a blush which was lost in the obscurity of the night. "And now, give me your two best horses to gain the second post."

"You shall have the two best horses, Aramis: and I again recommend Porthos strongly to you."

"Oh, have no fear on that head. One word more; do you think I am manoeuvring for him as I ought?"

"The evil being committed, yes; for the King would not pardon him, and you have, whatever may be said, always a supporter in M. Fouquet, who will not abandon you, he being himself compromised, notwithstanding his heroic action."

"You are right. And that is why, instead of gaining the sea at once, which would proclaim my fear and guilt, that is why I remain upon French ground. But Belle-Isle will be for me whatever ground I wish it to be—English, Spanish, or Roman; all will consist, with me, in the standard I shall think proper to unfurl."

"How so?"

"It was I who fortified Belle-Isle; and whilst I defend it, nobody can take Belle-Isle from me. And then, as you have said just now, M. Fouquet is there. Belle-Isle will not be attacked without the signature of M. Fouquet."

"That is true. Nevertheless, be prudent. The King is both cunning and strong." Aramis smiled.

"I again recommend Porthos to you," repeated the Comte, with a sort of cold persistence.

"Whatever becomes of me, Comte," replied Aramis, in the same tone, "our brother Porthos will fare as I do."

Athos bowed whilst pressing the hand of Aramis, and turned to embrace Porthos with much emotion.

"I was born lucky, was I not?" murmured the latter, transported with happiness, as he folded his cloak round him.

"Come, my dear friend," said Aramis.

18

In Which The Squirrel Falls—In Which The Adder Flies

It was two o'clock in the afternoon. The King, full of impatience, went to his cabinet on the terrace, and kept opening the door of the corridor, to see what his secretaries were doing. M. Colbert, seated in the same place M. Saint-Aignan had so long occupied in the morning, was chatting, in a low voice, with M. de Brienne. The King opened the door suddenly, and addressing them, "What do you say?" asked he.

"We were speaking of the first sitting of the States," said M. de Brienne, rising.

"Very well," replied the King, and returned to his room.

Five minutes after, the summons of the bell recalled Rose, whose hour it was.

"Have you finished your copies?" asked the King.

"Not yet, sire."

"See, then, if M. d'Artagnan has returned."

"Not yet, sire."

"It is very strange!" murmured the King. "Call M. Colbert."

Colbert entered; he had been expecting this moment all the morning.

"Monsieur Colbert," said the King very sharply; "it must be ascertained what has become of M. d'Artagnan."

Colbert, in his calm voice, replied, "Where would your Majesty desire him to be sought for?"

"Eh, monsieur, do you not know to what place I have sent him?" replied Louis acrimoniously.

"Your Majesty has not told me."

"Monsieur, there are things that are to be guessed; and you, above all others, do guess them. Have you not wondered why M. Fouquet is not with us?"

"I might have been able to imagine, sire; but I do not presume to be positive."

Colbert had not finished these words when a much rougher voice than that of the King interrupted the interesting conversation thus begun between the monarch and his clerk.

"D'Artagnan!" cried the King, with evident joy.

D'Artagnan, pale and in evidently bad humour, cried to the King, as he entered, "Sire, is it your Majesty who has given orders to my musketeers?"

"What orders?" said the King.

"About M. Fouquet's house?"

"None!" replied Louis.

"Ah, ah!" said d'Artagnan, biting his moustache; "I was not mistaken, then; it was monsieur, here;" and he pointed to Colbert.

"What orders? Let me know," said the King.

"Orders to turn a house inside out, to beat M. Fouquet's servants, to force the drawers, to give over a peaceful house to pillage! *Mordioux* ! These are savage orders!"

"Monsieur!" said Colbert, becoming pale.

"Monsieur!" interrupted d'Artagnan, "the King alone, understand—the King alone has a right to command my musketeers; but, as to you, I forbid you to do it, and I tell you so before His Majesty; gentlemen who wear swords are not fellows with pens behind their ears."

"D'Artagnan! d'Artagnan!" murmured the King.

"It is humiliating," continued the musketeer; "my soldiers are disgraced. I do not command a pack of pillagers, thank you, nor clerks of the intendance, *mordioux* !"

"Well, have you carried out my orders?" said the King, with authority.

"I have arrested M. Fouquet."

"You took plenty of time about it," said the King sharply. "Where is M. Fouquet at this moment?" he asked, after a short silence.

"M. Fouquet, sire," replied d'Artagnan, "is in the iron cage that M. Colbert had prepared for him, and is going, as fast as four vigorous horses can drag him, towards Angers."

"Why did you leave him on the road?"

"Because your Majesty did not tell me to go to Angers. The proof, the best proof of what I advance is that the King desired me to be sought for but this minute. And then I have another reason."

"What is that?"

"Whilst I was with him, poor M. Fouquet would never attempt to escape."

"Well!" cried the King, with stupefaction.

"Your Majesty ought to understand, and does understand certainly, that my warmest wish is to know that M. Fouquet is at liberty. I have given him one of my brigadiers, the most stupid I could find among my musketeers, in order that the prisoner might have a chance of escaping."

"Are you mad, Monsieur d'Artagnan!" cried the King, crossing his arms on his breast. "Do people speak such enormities, even when they have the misfortune to think them?"

"Ah, sire, you cannot expect that I should be the enemy of M. Fouquet, after what he has just done for you and me. No, no; if you desire that he should remain under your locks and bolts, never give him in charge to me; however closely wired might be the cage, the bird would, in the end, fly away."

"I am surprised," said the King in a stern voice, "you have not followed the fortunes of him whom M. Fouquet wished to place upon my throne. You had in him all you want—affection and gratitude. In my service, monsieur, you only find a master."

"If M. Fouquet had not gone to seek you in the Bastille,

sire," replied d'Artagnan, with a deeply impressive manner, "one single man would have gone there, and that man would have been me—you know that right well, sire."

The King was brought to a pause. Before that speech of his captain of the musketeers, so frankly spoken, and so true, the King had nothing to offer.

"Monsieur d'Artagnan," he said at last.

"Yes, sire."

"Give twenty of your musketeers to M. de Saint-Aignan, to form a guard for M. Fouquet."

D'Artagnan and Colbert exchanged looks. "And from Angers," continued the King, "they will conduct the prisoner to the Bastille, in Paris."

Saint-Aignan bowed, and departed to execute his commission.

D'Artagnan was about to retire likewise; but the King stopped him.

"Monsieur," said he, "you will go immediately, and take possession of the isle and fief of Belle-Isle-en-Mer."

"Yes, sire. Alone?"

"You will take a sufficient number of troops to prevent delay, in case the place should be rebellious."

A murmur of adulatory incredulity arose from the group of courtiers. "That is to be done," said d'Artagnan.

"I saw the place in my infancy," resumed the King, "and I do not wish to see it again. You have heard me? Go, monsieur, and do not return without the keys of the place."

Colbert went up to d'Artagnan. "A commission which, if you carry it out well," said he, "will be worth a marshal's baton to you."

"Why do you employ the words, 'if you carry it out well'?"

"Because it is difficult."

"Ah! In what respect?"

"You have friends in Belle-Isle, Monsieur d'Artagnan; and it is not an easy thing for men like you to march over the bodies of their friends to obtain success."

D'Artagnan hung down his head, whilst Colbert returned to the King. A quarter of an hour after, the captain received the written order from the King to blow up the fortress of Belle-Isle, in case of resistance, with the power of life and death over all the inhabitants or refugees, and an injunction not to allow one to escape.

"Colbert was right," thought d'Artagnan; "my baton of a marshal of France will cost the lives of my two friends. Only they seem to forget that my friends are not more stupid than the birds, and that they will not wait for the hand of the fowler to extend their wings. I will show them that hand so plainly, that they will have quite time enough to see it. Poor Porthos! Poor Aramis! No; my fortune shall not cost your wings a feather."

Having thus determined, d'Artagnan assembled the royal army, embarked it at Paimboeuf, and set sail, without losing a moment.

19

The Explanations Of Aramis

On Belle-Isle Aramis and Porthos waited in the early evening at the end of the mole. The sun had just gone down in the vast sheet of the reddened ocean. They held one another by the arm.

"What I have to say to you, friend Porthos, will probably surprise you, but it will instruct you."

"I like to be surprised," said Porthos in a kindly tone; "do not spare me therefore, I beg. I am hardened against emotions; don't fear, speak out."

"It is difficult, Porthos, it is—difficult; for, in truth, I warn you a second time, I have very strange things, very extraordinary things, to tell you."

"Oh, you speak so well, my friend, that I could listen to you for days together. Speak, then, I beg—and—stop, I have an idea; I will, to make your task more easy, I will, to assist you in telling me such things, question you."

"I shall be pleased at your doing so."

"What are we going to fight for, Aramis?"

"If you make me many such questions as that—if you would render my task the easier by interrupting my revelations thus, Porthos, you will not help me at all. So far, on the contrary, that is precisely the Gordian knot. But, my friend, with a man like you, good, generous, and devoted, the confession must be made bravely. I have deceived you, my worthy friend."

"You have deceived me!"

"Good Heavens, yes!"

"Was it for my good, Aramis?"

"I thought so, Porthos; I thought so sincerely, my friend."

"Then," said the honest seigneur of Bracieux, "you have rendered me a service, and I thank you for it; for if you had not deceived me, I might have deceived myself. In what, then, have you deceived me, say?"

"In that I was serving the usurper against whom Louis XIV, at this moment, is directing his efforts."

"The usurper!" said Porthos, scratching his head. "That is—well, I do not too clearly comprehend that."

"He is one of the two Kings who are contending for the crown of France."

"Very well! Then you were serving him who is not Louis XIV?"

"You have hit upon the matter in a word."

"It results that——"

"It results that we are rebels, my poor friend."

"The devil! The devil!" cried Porthos, much disappointed.

"Oh, but, dear Porthos, be calm; we shall still find means of getting out of the affair, trust me."

"It is not that which makes me uneasy," replied Porthos; "that which alone touches me is that ugly word *rebels* ."

"Ah, but—"

"And so, according to this, the duchy that was promised me—"

"It was the usurper who was to give it to you."

"And that is not the same thing, Aramis," said Porthos majestically.

"My friend, if it had only depended upon me, you should have become a prince." Porthos began to bite his nails after a melancholy fashion.

"That is where you have been wrong," continued he, "in deceiving me; for that promised duchy I reckoned upon. Oh! I reckoned upon it seriously, knowing you to be a man of your word, Aramis."

"Poor Porthos! Pardon me, I implore you!"

"So then," continued Porthos, without replying to the Bishop's prayer, "so then, it seems, I have quite fallen out with Louis XIV?"

"Oh, I will settle all that, my good friend, I will settle all that. I will take it upon myself alone!"

"Aramis !"

"No, no, Porthos, I conjure you, let me act. No false generosity! No inopportune devotedness! You knew nothing of my projects. You have done nothing of yourself. With me it is different. I am alone the author of the plot. I stood in need of my inseparable companion: I called upon you, and you came to me, in remembrance of our ancient device, 'All for one, one for all.' My crime was being an egotist."

"Now, that is a word I like," said Porthos; "and seeing that you have acted entirely for yourself, it is impossible for me to blame you; it is natural."

And upon this sublime reflection, Porthos pressed the hand of his friend cordially.

In presence of this ingenuous greatness of soul, Aramis felt himself little. It was the second time he had been compelled to bend before real superiority of heart, much more powerful than splendour of mind. He replied by a mute and energetic pressure to the kind endearment of his friend.

"Now," said Porthos, "that we have come to an explanation, now that I am perfectly aware of our situation with respect to Louis XIV, I think, my friend, it is time to make me comprehend the political intrigue of which we are the victims—for I plainly see there is a political intrigue at the bottom of all this."

"D'Artagnan, my good Porthos, d'Artagnan is coming, and will detail it to you in all its circumstances; but, excuse me, I am deeply grieved, I am bowed down by pain, and I have need of all my presence of mind, all my reflection, to extricate you from the false step in which I have so imprudently involved you; but nothing can be more clear, nothing more plain, than your position, henceforth. The King Louis XIV has no longer now but one enemy: that enemy is myself, myself alone. I have made you a prisoner, you have followed me, today I liberate you, you fly back to your prince. You can perceive, Porthos, there is not a single difficulty in all this."

"Do you think so?" said Porthos.

"I am quite sure of it."

"Then why," said the admirable good sense of Porthos, "then why, if we are in such an easy position, why, my friend, do we prepare cannon, muskets, and engines of all sorts? It seems to me it would be much more simple to say to Captain d'Artagnan: 'My dear friend, we have been mistaken; that error is to be repaired; open the door to us, let us pass through, and good-day!' "

"Ah, that!" said Aramis, shaking his head.

"Why do you say 'that'? Do you not approve of my plan, my friend?"

"I see a difficulty in it."

"What is it?"

"The hypothesis that d'Artagnan may come with orders which will oblige us to defend ourselves."

"What! Defend ourselves against d'Artagnan? Folly! Against the good d'Artagnan?"

Aramis once more replied by shaking his head.

"Porthos," at length said he, "if I have had the matches lighted and the guns pointed, if I have had the signal of alarm sounded, if I have called every man to his post upon the ramparts, those good ramparts of Belle-Isle which you have so well fortified, it is for something. Wait to judge; or rather, no, do not wait—"

"What can I do?"

"If I knew, my friend, I would have told you."

"But there is one thing much more simple than defending ourselves:—a boat, and away for France—where—"

"My dear friend," said Aramis, smiling with a strong

shade of sadness, "do not let us reason like children; let us be men in council and execution—But, hark! I hear a hail for landing at the port. Attention, Porthos, serious attention!"

"It is d'Artagnan, no doubt," said Porthos, in a voice of thunder, approaching the parapet.

"Yes, it is I," replied the captain of the musketeers running lightly up the steps of the mole, and gaining rapidly the little esplanade upon which his two friends waited for him. As soon as he came towards them, Porthos and Aramis observed an officer who followed d'Artagnan, treading apparently in his very steps. The captain stopped upon the stairs of the mole, when half-way up. His companion imitated him.

"Make your men draw back," cried d'Artagnan to Porthos and Aramis; "let them retire out of hearing." The order, being given by Porthos, was executed immediately. Then d'Artagnan, turning towards him who followed him:

"Monsieur," said he, "we are no longer here on board the King's fleet, where, in virtue of your order, you spoke so arrogantly to me just now."

"Monsieur," replied the officer, "I did not speak arrogantly to you; I simply, but rigorously, obeyed what I had been commanded. I have been directed to follow you. I follow you. I am directed not to allow you to communicate with any one without taking cognisance of what you do; I mix myself, therefore, with your communications."

D'Artagnan trembled with rage, and Porthos and Aramis, who heard this dialogue, trembled likewise, but with uneasiness and fear. D'Artagnan, biting his moustache with that vivacity which denoted in him the state of an exasperation closely to be followed by a terrible explosion, approached the officer.

"Monsieur," said he, in a low voice, so much the more impressive, that affecting a calm it threatened a tempest— "monsieur, when I sent a canoe hither, you wished to know what I wrote to the defenders of Belle-Isle. You produced an order to that effect; and, in my turn, I instantly showed you the note I had written. When the skipper of the boat sent by me returned, when I received the reply of these two gentlemen (and he pointed to Aramis and Porthos), you heard every word of what the messenger said. All that was plainly in your orders, all that was well executed, very punctually, was it not?"

"Yes, monsieur," stammered the officer; "yes, without doubt, but—"

"Monsieur," continued d'Artagnan, growing warm, "monsieur, when I manifested the intention of quitting my vessel to cross to Belle-Isle, you required to accompany me; I did not hesitate; I brought you with me. You are now at Belle-Isle, are you not?"

"Yes, monsieur, but—"

"But—the question no longer is of M. Colbert, who has given you that order, or of whomsoever in the world you are following the instructions: the question now is of a man who is a clog upon M. d'Artagnan, and who is alone with M. d'Artagnan upon steps whose feet are bathed by thirty feet of salt water; a bad position for that man, a bad position, monsieur! I warn you."

"But, monsieur, if I am a restraint upon you," said the officer timidly, and almost faintly, "it is my duty which—"

"Monsieur, you have had the misfortune, you or those who sent you, to insult me. It is done. I cannot seek redress from those who employ you—they are unknown to me, or are at too great a distance. But you are under my hand, and I swear that if you make one step behind me when I raise my feet to go up to those gentlemen—I swear to you by my name, I will cleave your head in two with my sword, and pitch you into the water. Oh, it will happen! It will happen! I have only been six times angry in my life, monsieur, and, on the five times which have preceded this, I have killed my man."

The officer did not stir; he became pale under this terrible threat, but replied with simplicity, "Monsieur, you are wrong in acting against my orders."

Porthos and Aramis, mute and trembling at the top of the parapet, cried to the musketeer, "Dear d'Artagnan, take care!"

D'Artagnan made them a sign to keep silence, raised his foot with a terrifying calmness to mount the stair, and turned round, sword in hand, to see if the officer followed him. The officer made a sign of the cross and stepped up. Porthos and Aramis, who knew their d'Artagnan, uttered a cry, and rushed down to prevent the blow they thought they already heard. But d'Artagnan, passing his sword into his left hand—

"Monsieur," said he to the officer in an agitated voice, "you are a brave man. You ought better to comprehend what I am going to say to you now than that which I have just said to you."

"Speak, Monsieur d'Artagnan, speak," replied the brave officer.

"These gentlemen we have just seen, and against whom you have orders, are my friends."

"I know they are, monsieur."

"You can understand if I ought to act towards them as your instructions prescribe."

"I understand your reserves."

"Very well; permit me, then, to converse with them without a witness?"

"Monsieur d'Artagnan, if I yielded to your request, if I did that which you beg me to do, I should break my word; but if I do not do it, I shall disoblige you. I prefer the one to the other. Converse with your friends, and do not despise me, monsieur, for doing for the sake of you, whom I esteem and honour; do not despise me for committing for you, and you alone, an unworthy act." D'Artagnan, much agitated, passed his arms rapidly round the neck of the young man, and went up to his friends. The officer, enveloped in his cloak, sat down on the damp weed-covered steps.

"Well," said d'Artagnan to his friends, "such is my position; judge for yourselves." They all three embraced. All three pressed each other in their arms as in the glorious days of their youth.

"What is the meaning of all these rigours?" said Porthos.

"You ought to have some suspicions of what it is," said d'Artagnan.

"Not much, I assure you, my dear captain; for, in fact, I have done nothing, no more has Aramis," hastened the worthy baron to say.

D'Artagnan darted a reproachful look at the prelate, which penetrated that hardened heart.

"Dear Porthos!" cried the Bishop of Vannes.

"You see what has been done against you," said d'Artagnan; "interception of all that is coming to or going from Belle-Isle. Your boats are all seized. If you had endeavoured to fly, you would have fallen into the hands of the cruisers which plough the sea in all directions on the watch for you. The King wants you to be taken, and he will take you." And d'Artagnan tore several hairs from his grey moustache. Aramis became sombre, Porthos angry.

"My idea was this," continued d'Artagnan; "to make you both come on board, to keep you near me, and restore you your liberty. But now, who can say that when I return to my ship, I may not find a superior; that I may not find secret orders which will take from me my command, and give it to another, who will dispose of me and you without hopes of help?"

"We must remain at Belle-Isle," said Aramis resolutely; "and I assure you, for my part, I will not surrender easily." Porthos said nothing. D'Artagnan remarked the silence of his friend.

"I have another trial to make of this officer, of this brave fellow who accompanies me, and whose courageous resistance makes me very happy; for it denotes an honest man, who, although an enemy, is a thousand times better than a complaisant coward. Let us try to learn from him what he has the right of doing, and what his orders permit or forbid."

"Let us try," said Aramis.

D'Artagnan came to the parapet, leaned over towards the steps of the mole, and called the officer, who immediately came up. "Monsieur," said d'Artagnan, after having exchanged the most cordial courtesies, natural between gentlemen, who know and appreciate each other worthily, "monsieur, if I wished to take away these gentlemen, what would you do?"

"I should not oppose it, monsieur; but having direct orders, formal orders to take them under my guard, I should detain them."

"Ah!" said d'Artagnan.

"That's all over," said Aramis gloomily. Porthos did not stir.

"But still take Porthos," said the Bishop of Vannes; "he can prove to the King, I will help him in doing so, and you also can, Monsieur d'Artagnan, that he has had nothing to do in this affair."

"Hum!" said d'Artagnan. "Will you come? Will you follow me, Porthos? The King is merciful."

"I beg to reflect," said Porthos nobly.

"You will remain here, then?"

"Until fresh orders," cried Aramis, with vivacity.

"Until we have had an idea," resumed d'Artagnan; "and I now believe that will not be long, for I have one already."

"Let us say *adieu*, then," said Aramis; "but in truth, my good Porthos, you ought to go."

"No!" said the latter laconically.

"As you please," replied Aramis, a little wounded in his nervous susceptibility at the morose tone of his companion. "Only I am reassured by the promise of an idea from d'Artagnan, an idea I fancy I have divined."

"Let us see," said the musketeer, placing his ear near Aramis's mouth. The latter spoke several words rapidly to which d'Artagnan replied, "That is it, precisely."

"Infallible, then!" cried Aramis.

"During the first emotion that this resolution will cause, take care of yourself, Aramis."

"Oh, don't be afraid."

"Now, monsieur," said d'Artagnan to the officer, "thanks, a thousand thanks! You have made yourself three friends for life."

"Yes," added Aramis. Porthos alone said nothing, but merely bowed.

D'Artagnan, having tenderly embraced his two old friends, left Belle-Isle with the inseparable companion M. Colbert had given him. Thus, with the exception of the explanation with which the worthy Porthos had been willing to be satisfied, nothing had changed in appearance in the fate of the one or the other. "Only," said Aramis, "there is d'Artagnan's idea."

D'Artagnan did not return on board without examining to the bottom the idea he had discovered. Now, we know that when d'Artagnan did examine, according to custom, daylight pierced through. As to the officer, become mute again, he left him full measure to meditate. Therefore, on putting his foot on board his vessel, moored within cannon-shot of the island, the captain of the musketeers had already got together all his means, offensive and defensive.

He immediately assembled his council, which consisted of the officers serving under his orders. These were eight in number: a chief of the maritime forces; a major directing the artillery; an engineer; the officer we are acquainted with; and four lieutenants. Having assembled them in the chamber of the poop, d'Artagnan arose, took off his hat, and addressed them thus:—

"Gentlemen, I have been to reconnoitre Belle-Isle-en-Mer, and I have found it a good and solid garrison; moreover, preparations are made for a defence that may prove troublesome. I therefore intend to send for two of the principal officers of the place, that we may converse with them. Having separated them from their troops and their cannon, we shall be better able to deal with them; particularly with good reasoning. Is this your opinion, gentlemen?"

The major of artillery rose.

"Monsieur," said he, with respect, but with firmness,"I have heard you say that the place is preparing to make a troublesome defence. The place is then, as you know, determined upon rebellion."

D'Artagnan was visibly put out by this reply; but he was not a man to allow himself to be subdued by so little, and resumed:—

"Monsieur," said he, "your reply is just. But you are ignorant that Belle-Isle is a fief of M. Fouquet's, and the ancient kings gave the right to the seigneurs of Belle-Isle to arm their people."

The major made a movement.

"Oh, do not interrupt me," continued d'Artagnan. "You are going to tell me that that right to arm themselves against the English was not a right to arm themselves against their king. But it is not M. Fouquet, I suppose, who holds Belle-Isle at this moment, since I arrested M. Fouquet the day before yesterday. Now the inhabitants and defenders of Belle-Isle know nothing of that arrest. You would announce it to them in vain. It is a thing so unheard-of and so extraordinary, so unexpected, that they would not believe you. A Breton serves his master, and not his masters; he serves his master till he has seen him dead. Now the Bretons, as far as I know, have not seen the body of M. Fouquet. It is not then surprising that they hold out against that which is not M. Fouquet or his signature."

The major bowed in sign of assent.

"That is why," continued d'Artagnan, "I propose to cause two of the principal officers of the garrison to come on board my vessel. They will see you, gentlemen; they will see the forces we have at our disposal; they will consequently know to what they have to trust, and the fate that attends them in case of rebellion. We will affirm to them, upon our honour, that M. Fouquet is a prisoner, and that all resistance can only be prejudicial to them. We will tell them that the first cannon that is fired, there will be no mercy to be expected from the King. Then, I hope at least, that they will no longer resist. They will yield without fighting, and we shall have a place given up to us in a friendly way, which it might cost us much trouble to subdue."

The officer who had followed d'Artagnan to Belle-Isle was preparing to speak, but d'Artagnan interrupted him.

"Yes, I know what you are going to tell me, monsieur; I know that there is an order of the King's to prevent all secret communications with the defenders of Belle-Isle, and that is exactly why I do not offer to communicate but in the presence of my staff."

And d'Artagnan made an inclination of the head to his officers, which had for its object attaching a value to that condescension.

The officers looked at each other as if to read their opinions in their eyes, with the intention of evidently acting, after they should have agreed, according to the desire of d'Artagnan. And already the latter saw with joy that the result of their consent would be sending a barque to Porthos and Aramis, when the King's officer drew from his pocket a folded paper, which he placed in the hands of d'Artagnan. The paper bore upon its superscription the number 1.

"What! More still!" murmured the suprised captain.

"Read, monsieur," said the officer, with a courtesy that was not free from sadness.

D'Artagnan, full of mistrust, unfolded the paper, and read these words:

"Prohibition to M. d'Artagnan to assemble any council

whatever, or to deliberate in any way before Belle-Isle be surrendered and the prisoners shot. Signed, LOUIS."

D'Artagnan repressed the movement of impatience that ran through his whole body, and, with a gracious smile,—

"That is well, monsieur," said he; "the King's orders shall be complied with."

20

Result Of The Ideas Of The King, And The Idea Of D'Artagnan

The blow was direct. It was severe, mortal. D'Artagnan, furious at having been anticipated by an idea of the King did not, however, yet despair; and, reflecting upon the idea he had brought back from Belle-Isle, he augured from it a new means of safety for his friends.

"Gentlemen," said he suddenly, "since the King has charged some other than myself with his secret orders, it must be because I no longer possess his confidence, and I should be really unworthy of it, if I had the courage to hold a command subject to so many injurious suspicions. I will go then immediately and carry my resignation to the King. I give it before you all, enjoining you all to fall back with me upon the coast of France, in such a way as not to compromise the safety of the forces His Majesty has confided to me. For this purpose, return all to your posts; within an hour we shall have the ebb of the tide. To your posts, gentlemen! I suppose," added he, on seeing that all prepared to obey him, except the surveillant officer, "you have no orders to object, this time?"

And d'Artagnan almost triumphed while speaking these words. This plan was the safety of his friends. The blockade once raised, they might embark immediately and set sail for England or Spain, without fear of being molested. Whilst they were making their escape, d'Artagnan would return to the King; would justify his return by the indignation which the mistrusts of Colbert had raised in him; he would be sent back with full powers, and he would take Belle-Isle, that is to say, the cage, after the birds had flown. But to this plan the officer opposed a second order of the King's. It was thus conceived:—

"From the moment M. d'Artagnan shall have manifested the desire of giving in his resignation, he shall no longer be reckoned leader of the expedition, and every officer placed under his orders shall be held to no longer obey him. Moreover, the said Monsieur d'Artagnan having lost that quality of leader of the army sent against Belle-Isle, shall set out immediately for France, in company of the officer who will have remitted the message to him, and who will consider him as a prisoner for whom he is answerable."

Brave and careless as he was, d'Artagnan turned pale. Everything had been calculated with a depth which, for the first time in thirty years, had recalled to him the solid foresight and the inflexible logic of the great Cardinal. He leant his head on his hand, thoughtful, scarcely breathing. "If I were to put this order into my pocket," thought he, "who would know it, or who would prevent my doing it? Before the King had had time to be informed, I should have saved those poor fellows yonder. Let us exercise a little audacity! My head is not one of those which the executioner strikes off for disobedience. We will disobey!" But at the moment he was about to adopt this plan, he saw the officers around him reading similar orders which the infernal agent of the thoughts of Colbert had just distributed to them. The case of disobedience had been foreseen, as the others had been.

"Monsieur," said the officer, coming up to him. "I await your good pleasure to depart."

"I am ready, monsieur," replied d'Artagnan, grinding his teeth.

The officer immediately commanded a canoe to receive M. d'Artagnan and himself. At sight of this he became almost mad with rage.

"How," stammered he, "will you carry on the direction of the different corps?"

"When you are gone, monsieur," replied the commander of the fleet, "it is to me the direction of the whole is committed."

"Then, monsieur," rejoined Colbert's man, addressing the new leader, "it is for you that this last order that has been remitted to me is intended. Let us see your powers."

"Here they are," said the sea officer, exhibiting a royal signature.

"Here are your instructions," replied the officer, placing the folded paper in his hands; and turning towards d'Artagnan, "Come, monsieur," said he in an agitated voice (such despair did he behold in that man of iron), "do me the favour to depart at once."

'Immediately!' articulated d'Artagnan feebly, subdued, crushed by implacable impossibility.

And he let himself slide down into the little boat, which started, favoured by wind and tide, for the coast of France. The King's guards embarked with him. The musketeer still preserved the hope of reaching Nantes quickly, and of pleading the cause of his friends eloquently enough to incline the King to mercy. The barque flew like a swallow. D'Artagnan distinctly saw the land of France profiled in black against the white clouds of night.

"Ah, monsieur," said he, in a low voice, to the officer, to whom, for an hour, he had ceased speaking, "what would I give to know the instructions for the new commander! They are all pacific, are they not? And—"

He did not finish; the sound of a distant cannon rolled over the waters, then another, and two or three still louder. D'Artagnan shuddered.

"The fire is opened upon Belle-Isle," replied the officer. The canoe had just touched the soil of France.

21

An Homeric Song

It is time to pass into the other camp. When d'Artagnan had
quitted them, Aramis turned suddenly to his companion.

"Dear Porthos," he said, "I will explain d'Artagnan's idea
to you. Did you remark, in the scene our friend had with the
officer, that certain orders restrained him with regard to us?"

"Yes. I did remark that."

"Well, d'Artagnan is going to give in his resignation to
the King, and during the confusion which will result from
his absence, we will get away." He paused as Porthos gazed
at him uncomprehendingly. "Remember, my friend, all the
world does not know of the grotto of Locmaria!"

"Ah, that is true!" cried Porthos joyously. "Now I comprehend. We are going to escape by the cavern."

"If you please," replied Aramis. "Forward, my friend.
There is much to be done before the landing of the royal
troops."

Some hours later, just after midnight had struck at the
fort, Porthos and Aramis loaded with money and arms,
walked hurriedly across the heath separating the mole and
the cavern. At length after a rapid course frequently interrupted by prudent stoppages, they reached the deep grotto
into which the foreseeing Bishop of Vannes had taken care
to have rolled upon cylinders a good barque capable of keeping the sea. The grotto extended the space of about two
hundred yards to a little creek dominating the sea, and they
hoped to roll the canoe to the water with the help of the
three Bretons who waited them beside the craft.

"Are all things ready, Yves?" asked the Bishop.

"Yes, monseigneur. Goenne is here, likewise his son who accompanies us."

"Good. On then, my 'good men'."

The three Bretons went to the boat and began to place the rollers underneath it. No sooner had they put it in motion than distant shouting from without made Aramis turn suddenly.

"Porthos," he cried, "our enemies are approaching!"

"Ah, ah!" said Porthos quietly, "what is to be done, then?"

"To commence combat," said Aramis, "is hazardous."

"Yes," said Porthos, "for it is difficult to suppose that out of two one should not be killed, and certainly, if one of us were killed, the other would get himself killed also." Porthos spoke these words with that heroic nature which, with him, grew greater with all the phases of the matter.

Aramis felt it like a spur to his heart. "We shall neither of us be killed if you do what I tell you, friend Porthos."

"Tell me what."

"These people are coming down into the grotto."

"Yes."

"We could kill about fifteen of them, but not more."

"If they fire all at once they will riddle us with balls."

"Without reckoning," added Aramis, "that the detonations might occasion fallings in of the cavern."

"Ay," said Porthos, "a piece of falling rock just now grazed my shoulder a little."

"You see, then!"

"Oh, it's nothing."

"We must determine upon something quickly. Our Bretons are going to continue to roll the canoe towards the sea."

"Very well."

"We two will keep the powder, the balls, and the muskets here."

"But only two, my dear Aramis—we shall never fire three shots together," said Porthos innocently; "the defence by musketry is a bad one."

"Find a better, then."

"I have found one," said the giant eagerly; "I will place myself in ambuscade behind the pillar with this iron bar, and invisible, unattackable if they come on in floods, I can let my bar fall upon their skulls, thirty times in a minute. *Hein*! What do you think of the project? You smile!"

"Excellent, dear friend, perfect! I approve it greatly; only you will frighten them, and half of them will remain outside to take us by famine. What we want, my good friend, is the entire destruction of the troop; a single man left standing ruins us."

"You are right, my friend, but how can we attract them, pray?"

"By not stirring, my good Porthos."

"Well, we won't stir, then; but when they shall be all together—"

"Then leave it to me! I have an idea."

"If it is thus, and your idea be a good one—and your idea is most likely to be good—I am satisfied."

"To your ambuscade, Porthos, and count how many enter."

"But you, what will you do?"

"Don't trouble yourself about me; I have a task to perform."

"I think I can hear cries."

"It is they. To your post. Keep within reach of my voice and hand."

Porthos took refuge in the second compartment, which was absolutely black with darkness. Aramis glided into the third; the giant held in his hand an iron bar of about fifty pounds weight. Porthos handled this lever, which had been used in rolling the barque, with marvellous facility. During this time, the Bretons had pushed the barque to the beach. In the enlightened compartment, Aramis, stooping and concealed, was busied in some mysterious manoeuvre. A command was given in a loud voice. It was the last order of the captain commandant. Twenty-five men jumped from the upper rocks into the first compartment of the grotto, and having taken their ground, began to fire. The echoes growled, the hissing of the balls cut the air, an opaque smoke filled the vault.

"To the left! To the left!" cried the leading officer, who, in his first assault, had seen the passage to the second chamber, and who, animated by the smell of powder, wished to guide his soldiers in that direction. The troop accordingly precipitated themselves to the left—the passage gradually growing narrower. The officer, with his hands stretched forward, devoted to death, marched in advance of the muskets. "Come on! Come on!" exclaimed he, "I see daylight!"

"Strike, Porthos!" cried the sepulchral voice of Aramis.

Porthos heaved a heavy sigh—but he obeyed. The iron bar fell full and direct upon the head of the officer, who was dead before he had ended his cry. Then the formidable lever rose ten times in ten seconds, and made ten corpses. The solders could see nothing; they heard sighs and groans; they stumbled over dead bodies, but as they had no conception of the cause of all this, they came forward jostling each other. The implacable bar, still falling, annihilated the first platoon, without a single sound having warned the second which was quietly advancing; only this second platoon, commanded by the captain, had broken a thin fir, growing on the shore, and, with its resinous branches twisted together, the captain had made a flambeau. On arriving at the compartment where Porthos, like the exterminating angel, had destroyed all he touched, the first rank drew back in terror. No firing had replied to that of the guards, and yet their way was stopped by a heap of dead bodies—they literally walked in blood. Porthos was still behind his pillar. The captain, on enlightening with the trembling flame of the fir this frightful carnage, of which he in vain sought the cause, drew back towards the pillar, behind which Porthos was concealed. Then a gigantic hand issued from the shade, and fastened on the throat of the captain, who uttered a stifled rattle; his outstretched arms beating the air, the torch fell and was extinguished in blood. A second after the corpse of the captain fell close to the extinguished torch, and added another body to the heap of dead which blocked up the passage. All this was effected as mysteriously as if by magic. At hearing the rattling in the throat of the captain, the soldiers who accompanied him had turned round; they had caught a glimpse of his extended arms, his eyes starting from their sockets, and then the torch fell and they were left in darkness. From an unreflective, instinctive, mechanical feeling, the lieutenant cried,—"Fire!"

Immediately a volley of musketry flamed, thundered, roared in the cavern, bringing down enormous fragments from the vaults. The cavern was lighted for an instant by this discharge, and then immediately returned to a darkness rendered still thicker by the smoke. To this succeeded a profound silence, broken only by the steps of the third brigade, now entering the cavern.

22

The Death Of A Titan

At the moment when Porthos, more accustomed to the darkness than all these men coming from open daylight, was looking round him to see if in this night Aramis were not making him some signal, he felt his arm gently touched, and a voice low as a breath murmured in his ear, "Come."

"Oh!" said Porthos.

"Hush!" said Aramis, if possible, still more softly.

And amidst the noise of the third brigade, which continued to advance, amidst the imprecations of the guards left alive, of the dying, rattling their last sigh, Aramis and Porthos glided imperceptibly along the granite walls of the cavern. Aramis led Porthos into the last but one compartment, and showed him, in a hollow of the rocky wall, a barrel of powder weighing from seventy to eighty pounds, to which he had just attached a match, "My friend," said he to Porthos, "you will take this barrel, the match of which I am going to set fire to, and throw it amidst our enemies; can you do so?"

"*Parbleu* !" replied Porthos; and he lifted the barrel with one hand. "Light it!"

"Stop," said Aramis, "till they are all massed together, and then, my Jupiter, hurl your thunderbolt among them."

"Light it," repeated Porthos.

"On my part," continued Aramis, "I will join our Bretons, and help them to get the canoe to the sea. I will wait for you on the shore; launch it strongly, and hasten to us."

"Light it," said Porthos, a third time.

"But do you understand me?"

"*Parbleu* !" said Porthos again, with laughter that he did not even attempt to restrain; "when a thing is explained to me I understand it; begone, and give me the light."

Aramis gave the burning match to Porthos, who held out his arm to him, his hands being engaged. Aramis pressed the arm of Porthos with both his hands, and fell back to the outlet of the cavern where the three rowers awaited him.

Porthos, left alone, applied the spark bravely to the match. The spark,—a feeble spark, first principle of a conflagration—shone in the darkness like a firefly, then was deadened against the match which it enflamed, Porthos enlivening the flame with his breath. The smoke was a little dispersed, and by the light of the sparkling match, objects might, for two seconds, be distinguished. It was a short but a splendid spectacle, that of this giant, pale, bloody, his countenance lighted by the fire of the match burning in surrounding darkness! The soldiers saw him—they saw the barrel he held in his hand—they at once understood what was going to happen. Then, these men, already filled with terror at the sight of what had been accomplished—filled with terror at thinking of what was going to be accomplished, threw forth together one shriek of agony. Some endeavoured to fly, but they encountered the third brigade, which barred their passage; others mechanically took aim, and attempted to fire their discharged muskets; others fell upon their knees. Two or three officers cried out to Porthos to promise him his liberty if he would spare their lives. The lieutenant of the third brigade commanded his men to fire; but the guards had before them their terrified companions, who served as a living rampart for Porthos. We have said that the light produced by the spark and the match did not last more than two seconds; but during these two seconds this is what it illuminated—in the first place, the giant, enlarging in the darkness; then, at ten paces from him, a heap of bleeding bodies, crushed, mutilated, in the midst of whom still lived some last struggle of agony, which lifted the mass as a last respiration raises the sides of a shapeless monster expiring in the night. Every breath of Porthos, whilst enlivening the match, sent towards this heap of bodies a sulphurous hue mingled with streaks of purple. In addition to this principal group, scattered about the grotto, as the chance of death or the surprise of the blow had stretched them, some isolated bodies seemed to threaten by their gaping wounds. Above the ground, soaked by pools of blood, rose heavy and sparkling, the short, thick pillars of the cavern, of which the strongly marked shades threw out the luminous particles. And all this was seen by the tremulous light of a match attached to a barrel of powder; that is to say, a torch which, whilst throwing a light upon the dead past, showed the death to come.

As I have said, this spectacle did not last above two seconds. During this short space of time an officer of the third brigade got together eight men armed with muskets; and, through an opening, ordered them to fire upon Porthos. But they who received the order to fire trembled so, that three guards fell by the discharge, and the five other balls went hissing to splinter the vault, plough the ground, or indent the sides of the cavern.

A burst of laughter replied to this volley; then the arm of the giant swung round; then was seen to pass through the air, like a falling star, the train of fire. The barrel, hurled a distance of thirty feet, cleared the barricade of dead bodies, and fell amidst a group of shrieking soldiers, who threw themselves on their faces. The officer had followed the brilliant train in the air; he endeavoured to precipitate himself upon the barrel and tear out the match before it reached the powder it contained. Useless devotedness! The air had made the flame attached to the conductor more active; the match, which at rest might have burnt five minutes, was consumed in thirty seconds, and the infernal work exploded. Furious vortices, hissings of sulphur and nitre, devouring ravages of the fire which caught to objects, the terrible thunder of the explosion, this is what the second which followed the two seconds we have described, disclosed in that cavern, equal in horrors to a cavern of demons. The rock split like planks of deal under the axe. A jet of fire, smoke, and debris sprang up from the middle of the grotto, enlarging as it mounted. The large walls of silex tottered and fell upon the sand, and the sand itself, an instrument of pain when launched from its hardened bed, riddled the face with its myriads of cutting atoms. Cries, howlings, imprecations, and existences—all were extinguished in one immense crash.

The three first compartments became a gulf into which fell back again, according to its weight, every vegetable, mineral, or human fragment. Then the lighter sand and ashes fell in their turn, stretching like a grey winding sheet and smoking over these dismal funerals. And now, seek in this burning tomb, in this subterraneous volcano, seek for the King's guards with their blue coats laced with silver. Seek for the officers brilliant in gold; seek for the arms upon which they depended for their defence; seek for the stones that have killed them, the ground that has borne them. One single man has made of all this a chaos more confused, more shapeless, more terrible than the chaos which existed an hour before God had created the world. There remained nothing of the three compartments—nothing by which God could have known His own work. As to Porthos, after having hurled the barrel of powder amidst his enemies, he had fled as Aramis had directed him to do, and had gained the last compartment, into which air, light, and sunshine penetrated through the opening. Therefore, scarcely had he turned the angle which separated the third compartment from the fourth when he perceived at a hundred paces from him the barque dancing on the waves; there were his friends, there was liberty, there was life after victory. Six more of his formidable strides, and he would be out of the vault; out of the vault! Two or three vigorous springs and he would reach the canoe. Suddenly he felt his knees give way; his knees appeared powerless, his legs to yield under him.

"Oh! oh!" murmured he, "there is my fatigue seizing me again! I can walk no farther! What is this?"

Aramis perceived him through the opening, and unable to conceive what could induce him to stop thus—"Come on, Porthos! Come on!" cried he; "come quickly."

"Oh!" replied the giant, making an effort which acted upon every muscle of his body—"oh, but I cannot." While saying these words he fell upon his knees, but with his robust hands he clung to the rocks, and raised himself up again.

"Quick! quick!" repeated Aramis, bending forward towards the shore, as if to draw Porthos towards him with his arms.

"Here I am," stammered Porthos, collecting all his strength to make one step more.

"In the name of Heaven, Porthos, make haste! The barrel will blow up!"

"Make haste, monseigneur!" shouted the Bretons to Porthos, who was floundering as in a dream.

But there was no longer time; the explosion resounded, the earth gaped, the smoke which rushed through the large fissures obscured the sky; the sea flowed back as if driven by the blast of fire which darted from the grotto as if from the jaws of a gigantic chimera; the reflux carried the barque out twenty yards; the rocks cracked to their base, and separated like blocks beneath the operation of wedges; a portion of the vault was carried up towards heaven, as if by rapid currents; the rose-coloured and green fire of the sulphur, the black lava of the argillaceous liquefactions clashed and combated for an instant beneath a majestic dome of smoke; then, at first oscillated, then declined, then fell successively the long angles of rock which the violence of the explosion had not been able to uproot from their bed of ages; they bowed to each other like grave and slow old men, then prostrated themselves, embedded for ever in their dusty tomb.

This frightful shock seemed to restore to Porthos the strength he had lost; he arose, himself a giant among these giants. But at the moment he was flying between the double hedge of granite phantoms, these latter, which were no longer supported by the corresponding links, began to roll with a crash around this Titan, who looked as if precipitated from heaven amidst rocks which he had just been launching at it. Porthos felt the earth beneath his feet shaken by this long rending. He extended his vast hands to the right and left to repulse the falling rocks. A gigantic block was held back by each of his extended hands; he bent his head and a third granite mass sank between his two shoulders. For an instant the arms of Porthos had given way, but the Hercules united all his forces, and the two walls of the prison in which he was buried fell back slowly and gave him place. For an instant he appeared in this frame of granite like the ancient angel of chaos, but in pushing back the lateral rocks, he lost his point of support for the monolith, which weighed upon his strong shoulders, and the monolith, weighing upon him with all its weight, brought the giant down upon his knees. The lateral rocks, for an instant pushed back, drew together again, and added their weight to the primitive weight which would have been sufficient to crush ten men. The giant fell without crying for help; he fell while answering Aramis with words of encouragement and hope, and, thanks to the powerful arch of his hands, for an instant, he might believe that, like Enceladus, he should shake off the triple load. But, by degrees, Aramis saw the block sink; the hands strung for an instant, the arms stiffened for a last effort, gave way, the extended shoulders sank wounded and torn, and the rock continued to lower gradually.

"Porthos! Porthos!" cried Aramis, tearing his hair. "Porthos, where are you? Speak!"

"There, there!" murmured Porthos, with a voice growing evidently weaker, "Patience! Patience!"

Scarcely had he pronounced these words, when the impulse of the fall augmented the weight; the enormous rock sat down, pressed by the two others which sank in from the sides, and, as it were, swallowed up Porthos in a sepulchre of broken stones. On hearing the dying voice of his friend, Aramis had sprung to land. Two of the Bretons followed him, with each a lever in his hand—one being sufficient to take care of the barque. The last rattles of the valiant struggler guided them amidst the ruins. Aramis, animated, active, and young as at twenty, sprang towards the triple mass, and with his hands, delicate as those of a woman, raised by a miracle of vigour a corner of the immense sepulchre of granite. Then he caught a glimpse, in the darkness of that grave, of the still brilliant eye of his friend, to whom the momentary lifting of the mass restored that moment of respiration. The two men came rushing in, grasped their iron levers, united their triple strength, not merely to raise it, but to sustain it. All was useless. The three men slowly gave way with cries of grief, and the rough voice of Porthos, seeing them exhaust themselves in a useless struggle, murmured in a jeering tone those supreme words which came to his lips with the last respiration, "Too heavy."

After which the eye darkened and closed, the face became pale, the hand whitened, and the Titan sank quite down, breathing his last sigh. With him sank the rock, which, even in his agony, he had still held up. The three men dropped the levers, which rolled upon the tumulary stone. Then, breathless, pale, his brow covered with sweat, Aramis listened, his breast oppressed, his heart ready to break.

Nothing more! The giant slept the eternal sleep, in the sepulchre which God had made to his measure.

23

The Epitaph Of Porthos

Aramis, silent, icy, trembling like a timid child, arose shivering from the stone. A Christian does not walk upon tombs. But though capable of standing, he was not capable of walking. It might be said that something of dead Porthos had just died within him. His Bretons surrounded him; Aramis yielded to their kind exertions, and the three sailors, lifting him up, carried him into the canoe. Then having laid him down upon the bench near the rudder, they took to their oars, preferring to get off by rowing to hoisting a sail, which might betray them.

Of all that levelled surface of the ancient grotto of Locmaria, of all that flattened shore, one single little hillock attracted their eyes. Aramis never removed his from it; and, at a distance out in the sea, in proportion as the shore receded, the menacing and proud mass of rock seemed to draw itself up, as formerly Porthos used to draw himself up, and raise a smiling and invincible head towards heaven, like that of the honest and valiant friend, the strongest of the four, and yet the first dead. Strange destiny of these men of brass! The most simple of heart allied to the most crafty; strength of body guided by subtlety of mind; and in the decisive moment, when vigour alone could save mind and body, a stone, a rock, a vile and material weight, triumphed over vigour, and falling upon the body drove out the mind.

Worthy Porthos! Born to help other men, always ready to sacrifice himself for the safety of the weak, as if God had only given him strength for that purpose; when dying he only thought he was carrying out the conditions of his compact with Aramis, a compact, however, which Aramis alone had drawn up, and which Porthos had only known to suffer by its terrible solidarity. Noble Porthos! Of what good are the châteaux overflowing with sumptuous furniture, the forests overflowing with game, the lakes overflowing with fish, the cellars overflowing with wealth! Of what good are the lackeys in brilliant liveries, and in the midst of them, Mousqueton, proud of the power delegated by thee! Oh, noble Porthos! Careful heaper up of treasures, was it worth while to labour to sweeten and gild life, to come upon a desert shore, to the cries of sea birds, and lay thyself, with broken bones, beneath a cold stone? Was it worth while, in short, noble Porthos, to heap so much gold, and not have even the distich of a poor poet engraven upon thy monument? Valiant Porthos! He still, without doubt, sleeps, lost, forgotten, beneath the rock which the shepherds of the heath take for the mighty roof-stone of a sunken cromlech. And so many twining brambles, so many mosses, caressed by the bitter wind of the ocean, so many vivacious lichens have soldered the sepulchre to the earth, that the passenger will never imagine that such a block of granite can ever have been supported by the shoulders of one man.

Aramis, still pale, still icy, his heart upon his lips, Aramis looked, even till, with the last ray of daylight, the shore faded on the horizon. Not a word escaped his lips, not a sigh rose from his deep breast. The superstitious Bretons looked at him trembling. That silence was not of a man, it was of a statue. In the meantime, with the first grey lines that descended from the heavens, the canoe had hoisted its little sail, which, swelling with the kisses of the breeze, and carrying them rapidly from the coast, made brave way with its head towards Spain, across the terrible gulf of Gascony, so rife with tempests. But scarcely half an hour after the sail had been hoisted, the rowers became inactive, reclining upon their benches and, making an eyeshade with their hands, pointed out to each other a white spot which appeared on the horizon as motionless as is in appearance a gull rocked by the insensible respiration of the waves. But that which might have appeared motionless to ordinary eyes was moving at a quick rate to the experienced eye of the sailor; that which appeared stationary on the ocean was cutting a rapid way through it. For some time, seeing the profound torpor in which their master was plunged, they did not dare to rouse him, and satisfied themselves with exchanging their conjectures in a low, disturbed voice. Aramis, in fact, so vigilant, so active—Aramis, whose eye, like that of the lynx, watched without ceasing, and saw better by night than by day— Aramis seemed to sleep in the despair of his soul. An hour passed thus, during which daylight gradually disappeared, but during which also the sail in view gained so swiftly on the barque, that Goenne, one of the three sailors, ventured to say aloud,—

"Monseigneur, we are being chased!"

Aramis made no reply; the ship still gained upon them. Then, of their own accord, two of the sailors, by the direction of the skipper Yves, lowered the sail, in order that that single point which appeared above the surface of the waters should cease to be a guide to the eye of the enemy who was pursuing them. On the part of the ship in sight, on the contrary, two more small sails were run up at the extremities of the masts. Unfortunately, it was the time of the finest and longest days of the year, and the moon in all her brilliancy succeeded to this inauspicious daylight. The corvette, which was pursuing the little barque before the wind, had then still half an hour of twilight, and a whole night almost as light as day.

"Monseigneur, monseigneur, we are lost!" said the skipper; "Look! They see us although we have lowered our sail."

"That is not to be wondered at," murmured one of the sailors, "since they say that, by the aid of the devil, the people of the cities have fabricated instruments with which they see as well at a distance as near, by night as well as by day."

Aramis took a telescope from the bottom of the boat, arranged it silently, and passing it to the sailor: "Here," said he, "look!" The sailor hesitated.

"Don't be alarmed," said the Bishop, "there is no sin in it; and if there is any sin, I will take it upon myself."

The sailor lifted the glass to his eye and uttered a cry. He believed that the vessel, which appeared to be distant about cannon-shot, had suddenly and at a single bound cleared the distance. But, on withdrawing the instrument from his eye, he saw that, except the way which the corvette had been able to make during that short instant, it was still at the same distance.

"So," murmured the sailor, "they can see us as we see them."

"They see us," said Aramis, and sank again into his impassibility.

"How—they see us!" said Yves, "impossible!"

"Well, look yourself," said the sailor. And he passed the glass to the skipper.

"Monseigneur assures me that the devil has nothing to do with this?" asked the skipper. Aramis shrugged his shoulders.

The skipper lifted the glass to his eye. "Oh, monseigneur," said he, "it is a miracle—they are there; it seems as if I were going to touch them. Twenty-five men at least! Ah! I see the captain forward. He holds a glass like this, and is looking at us. Ah, he turns round, and gives an order; they are rolling a piece of cannon forward—they are charging it—they are pointing it. *Miséricorde* ! They are firing at us."

And by a mechanical movement, the skipper took the glass off, and the objects, sent back to the horizon, appeared again in their true aspect. The vessel was still at the distance of nearly a league, but the manoeuvre announced by the skipper was not less real. A light cloud of smoke appeared under the sails, more blue than they, and spreading like a flower opening; then, at about a mile from the little canoe, they saw the ball take the crown off two or three waves, dig a white furrow in the sea, and disappear at the end of that furrow, as inoffensive as the stone with which, at play, a boy makes ducks and drakes. That was at once a menace and a warning.

"What is to be done?" asked the skipper.

"They will sink us!" cried Goenne. "Give us absolution, monseigneur!" And the sailors fell on their knees before him.

"You forget that they can see you," said he.

"That is true," said the sailors, ashamed of their weakness. "Give us your orders, monseigneur; we are ready to die for you."

"Let us wait," said Aramis.

"How—let us wait?"

"Yes; do you not see, as you just now said, that if we endeavour to fly, they will sink us."

"But, perhaps," the skipper ventured to say, "perhaps by the favour of the night we could escape them."

"Oh," said Aramis, "they have, little doubt, some Greek fire to lighten their own course and ours likewise."

At the same moment, as if the little vessel wished to reply to the appeal of Aramis, a second cloud of smoke mounted slowly to the heavens, and from the bosom of that cloud sparked an arrow of flame, which described its parabola like a rainbow, and fell into the sea, where it continued to burn, illuminating a space of a quarter of a league in diameter.

The Bretons looked at each other in terror. "You see plainly," said Aramis, "it will be better to wait for them."

The oars dropped from the hands of the sailors, and the barque, ceasing to make way, rocked motionless on the summits of the waves. Night came on, but the vessel still approached nearer. It might be said it redoubled its speed with the darkness. From time to time, as a bloody-necked vulture rears its head out of its nest, the formidable Greek fire darted from its sides, and cast its flame into the ocean like an incandescent snow. At last it came within musket-shot. All the men were on deck, arms in hand; the cannoniers were at their guns, and matches were burning. It might be thought they were about to board a frigate and to combat a crew superior in number to their own, and not to take a canoe manned by four people.

"Surrender!" cried the commander of the corvette, with the aid of the speaking trumpet.

The sailors looked at Aramis. Aramis made a sign with his head. Yves waved a white cloth at the end of a gaff. This was like striking their flag. The vessel came on like a race-horse. It launched a fresh Greek fire which fell within twenty paces of the little canoe, and threw a stronger light upon them than the most ardent ray of the sun could have done.

"At the first sign of resistance," cried the commander of the corvette, "fire!" And the soldiers brought their muskets to the present.

"Did not we say we surrendered?" said Yves.

"Living ! Living, captain!" cried some highly excited soldiers. "They must be taken living."

"Well, yes—living," said the captain. Then turning towards the Bretons, "Your lives are all safe, my friends," cried he, "except the Chevalier d'Herblay."

Aramis started imperceptibly. For an instant his eye was fixed upon the depths of the ocean enlightened by the last flashes of the Greek fire, flashes which ran along the sides of the waves, played upon their crests like plumes, and rendered still more dark, more mysterious and more terrible the abysses they covered.

"Do you hear, monseigneur?" said the sailors.

"Yes."

"What are your orders?"

"Accept!"

"But you, monseigneur!"

Aramis leant still more forward, and played with the ends of his long white fingers with the green water of the sea, to which he turned smiling as a friend.

"Accept!" he repeated.

"We accept," repeated the sailors; "but what security have we?"

"The word of a gentleman," said the officer. "By my rank and by my name I swear, that all but M. le Chevalier d'Herblay shall have their lives spared. I am lieutenant of the King's frigate the *Pomona*, and my name is Louis Constant de Pressigny."

With a rapid gesture, Aramis—already bent over the side of the barque towards the sea—with a rapid gesture, Aramis raised his head, drew himself up, and with a flashing eye, and a smile upon his lips, "Throw out the ladder, messieurs," said he, as if the command had belonged to him. He was obeyed. Then Aramis seized the rope-ladder, and the surprise of the sailors of the corvette was great, when they saw him walk straight up to the commander with a firm step, look at him earnestly, make a sign to him with his hand, a mysterious and unknown sign, at the sight of which the officer turned pale, trembled, and bowed his head. Without saying a word, Aramis then raised his hand close to the eyes of the commander, and showed him the collet of a ring which he wore on the ring-finger of his left hand. And while making this sign, Aramis, draped in cold, silent, and haughty majesty, had the air of an emperor giving his hand to be kissed. The commandant, who for a moment had raised his head, bowed a second time with marks of the most profound respect. Then, stretching his hand out towards the poop, that is to say, towards his own cabin, he drew back to allow Aramis to go first. The three Bretons, who had come on board after their Bishop, looked at each other, stupefied. The crew were struck with silence. Five minutes after, the commander called the second lieutenant, who returned immediately, and gave directions for the head to be put towards Corunna. Whilst the order was being executed Aramis reappeared upon the deck, and took a seat near the bulwarks. The night had fallen, the moon had not yet risen, and yet Aramis looked incessantly towards Belle-Isle. Yves then approached the captain, who had returned to take his post in the stern, and said, in a low and humble voice, "What course are we to follow, captain?"

"We take what course monseigneur pleases," replied the officer.

Aramis passed the night leaning upon the bulwarks. Yves, on approaching him the next morning, remarked, that "the night must have been very humid, for the wood upon which the Bishop's head had rested, was soaked with dew." Who knows? That dew was, perhaps, the first tears that had ever fallen from the eyes of Aramis!

What epitaph would have been worth that, good Porthos?

24

The Angel Of Death

A horse was heard galloping over the hard gravel of the great alley of the Château of Athos at Blois, and the sound of most noisy and animated conversations ascended to the chamber in which the Comte was dreaming of his beloved son, Raoul. Athos did not stir from the place he occupied; he scarcely turned his head towards the door to ascertain the sooner what these noises could be. A heavy step ascended the stairs; the horse which had recen'y galloped, departed slowly towards the stables. Great hesitation appeared in the steps, which by degrees approached the chamber of Athos. A door then was opened, and Athos, turning a little towards the part of the room the noise came from, cried in a weak voice:—

"It is a courier from Africa, is it not?"

"No, Monsieur le Comte," replied a voice which made the father of Raoul start upright in his bed.

"Grimaud!" murmured he, and the sweat began to pour down his cheeks. Grimaud appeared in the door-way, a stern and pale old man, his clothes covered with dust, with a few scattered hairs whitened by old age. He trembled whilst leaning against the door-frame, and was near falling on seeing, by the light of the lamps, the countenance of his master. These two men, who had lived so long together in a community of intelligence, and whose eyes, accustomed to economise expressions, knew how to say so many things silently—these two old friends, one as noble as the other in heart, if they were unequal in fortune and birth, remained interdicted whilst looking at each other. By the exchange of a single glance, they had just read to the bottom of each other's hearts. Grimaud bore upon his countenance the impression of a grief already old, of a dismal familiarity with it. He appeared to have no longer in use but one single version of his thoughts. As formerly he was accustomed not to speak much, he was now accustomed not to smile at all. Athos read at a glance all these shades upon the visage of his faithful servant, and in the same tone he would have employed to speak to Raoul in his dream—

"Grimaud," said he, "Raoul is dead, is he not?"

Behind Grimaud, the other servants listened breathlessly with their eyes fixed upon the bed of their sick master. They heard the terrible question, and an awful silence ensued.

"Yes," replied the old man, heaving up the monosyllable from his chest with a hoarse, broken sigh.

Then arose voices of lamentation, which groaned without measure, and filled with regrets and prayers the chamber where the agonised father sought with his eyes for the portrait of his son. This was for Athos like the transition which led to his dream. Without uttering a cry, without shedding a tear, patient, mild, resigned as a martyr, he raised his eyes towards heaven, in order to there see again, rising above the mountain of Gigelli, the beloved shade which was leaving him at the moment of Grimaud's arrival. Without doubt, while looking towards the heavens, when resuming his marvellous dream, he repassed by the same road by which the vision, at once so terrible and so sweet, had led him before, for, after having gently closed his eyes, he reopened them and began to smile; he had just seen Raoul, who had smiled upon him. With his hands joined upon his breast, his face turned towards the window, bathed by the fresh air of night, which brought to his pillow the aroma of the flowers and the woods, Athos entered, never again to come out of it, into the contemplation of that paradise which the living never see. God willed, no doubt, to open to this elect the treasures of eternal beatitude, at the hour when other men tremble with the idea of being severely received by the Lord, and cling to this life they know, in the dread of the other life of which they get a glimpse by the dismal, murky torches of death. Athos was guided by the pure and serene soul of his son, which aspired to be like the paternal soul. Everything for this just man was melody and perfume in the rough road which souls take to return to the celestial country. After an hour of this ecstasy, Athos softly raised his hands, as white as wax; the smile did not quit his lips, and he murmured low, so low as scarcely to be audible, these three words addressed to God or to Raoul:

"HERE I AM!"

And his hands fell down slowly, as if he himself had laid them on the bed.

Death had been kind and mild to this noble creature. It had spared him the tortures of the agony, the convulsions of the last departure; it had opened with an indulgent finger the gates of eternity to that noble soul, worthy of every respect. God had no doubt ordered it thus that the pious remembrance of this death should remain in the hearts of those present, and in the memory of other men—a death which caused to be loved the passage from this life to the other by those whose existence upon this earth leads them not to dread the last judgment. Athos preserved, even in the eternal sleep, that placid and sincere smile—an ornament which was to accompany him to the tomb. The quietude of his features, the calm of his nothingness, made his servants for a long time doubt whether he had really quitted life. The Comte's people wished to remove Grimaud, who, from a distance, devoured the face growing so pale, and did not approach, from the pious fear of bringing to him the breath of death. But Grimaud, fatigued as he was, refused to leave the room. He sat himself down upon the threshold, watching his master with the vigilance of a sentinel, and jealous to receive either his first waking look, or his last dying sigh. The noises were all quieted in the house, and every one respected the slumber of their lord. But Grimaud, by anxiously listening, perceived that the Comte no longer breathed. He raised himself, with his hands leaning on the ground, looked to see if there did not appear some motion in the body of his master. Nothing! Fear seized him; he rose completely up, and, at the very moment, heard some one coming up the stairs. A noise of spurs knocking against a sword—a warlike sound, familiar to his ears— stopped him as he was going towards the bed of Athos. A voice still more sonorous than brass or steel resounded within three paces of him.

"Athos ! Athos, my friend !" cried this voice, agitated even to tears.

"Monsieur le Chevalier d'Artagnan!" faltered out Grimaud.

"Where is he? Where is he?" continued the musketeer.

Grimaud seized his arm in his bony fingers, and pointed to the bed, upon the sheets of which the livid tint of the dead already showed.

A choked respiration, the opposite to a sharp cry, swelled the throat of d'Artagnan. He advanced on tiptoe, trembling, frightened at the noise his feet made upon the floor, and his heart rent by a nameless agony. He placed his ear to the breast of Athos, his face to the Comte's mouth. Neither noise, nor breath! D'Artagnan drew back. Grimaud, who had followed him with his eyes, and for whom each of his movements had been a revelation, came timidly, and seated himself at the foot of the bed, and glued his lips to the sheet which was raised by the stiffened feet of his master. Then large drops began to flow from his red eyes. This old man in despair, who wept, bent double without uttering a word, presented the most moving spectacle that d'Artagnan, in a life so filled with emotion, had ever met with.

The captain remained standing in contemplation before that smiling dead man, who seemed to have kept his last thought to make to his best friend, to the man he had loved next to Raoul, a gracious welcome even beyond life; and as if to reply to that exalted flattery of hospitality, d'Artagnan went and kissed Athos fervently on the brow, and with his trembling fingers closed his eyes. Then he seated himself by the pillow without dread of that dead man, who had been so kind and affectionate to him for thirty-five years; he fed himself greedily with the remembrances which the noble visage of the Comte brought to his mind in crowds—some blooming and charming as that smile—some dark, dismal, and icy as that face with its eyes closed for eternity.

His thoughts went out to his other two friends and to all that had happened since that sorrowful evening when he had parted from them at Belle-Isle. His own fate had surprised him. Having returned as planned to offer the King his resignation, he had been delighted to find that not only was Louis unwilling to accept it but anxious for him to win his Marshal's baton fighting France's enemies on foreign soil. The King had added further to d'Artagnan's joy by telling him that pardon was likewise granted to Aramis and Porthos, and that it would be his glad duty to return to Belle-Isle and tell them so. A bitter blow it had been then for him to learn there that his dear friend Porthos lay buried deep—in the grotto of Locmaria and far beyond the reach of pardon. Even the knowledge that Aramis had persuaded his captors to carry him safely to Spain and that the two brave musketeers had caused the loss of one hundred and ten of the royal troops had failed to console d'Artagnan in his grief.

Now, as he gazed on the dear face of Athos, the second friend now taken from him, the bitter flood which mounted from minute to minute invaded his heart, and swelled his breast almost to bursting. Incapable of mastering his emotion, he rose, and tearing himself violently from the chamber where he had just found dead him to whom he came to report the news of the death of Porthos, he uttered sobs so heart-rending that the servants who seemed only to wait for an explosion of grief, answered to it by their lugubrious clamours, and the dogs of the late Comte by their lamentable howlings. Grimaud was the only one who did not lift up his voice. Even in the paroxysm of his grief he would not have dared to profane the dead, or for the first time disturb the slumber of his master. Athos had accustomed him never to speak.

At daybreak, d'Artagnan, who had wandered about the lower hall, biting his fingers to stifle his sighs, went up once more, followed by the faithful Grimaud, who made no more noise than a shadow. Then, going down again, he went outside alone to walk about in the first blue rays of day, in the dark alley of old limes, marked by the still visible footprints of the Comte who had just died.

Epilogue

Four years after the scene we have just described, d'Artagnan was seated at the King's table. Near him were M. Colbert and M. le Duc d'Alméda, none other than our old friend Aramis, now Spanish ambassador to the French court. The King was very gay and paid a thousand little attentions to the Queen. It might have been supposed to be that calm time when the King used to watch the eyes of his mother for the avowal or disavowal of what he had just done.

During this time Colbert was talking with the Duc d'Alméda.

"Monsieur," said Colbert to Aramis, "this is the moment for us to come to an understanding. I have made your peace with the King, and I owed that clearly to a man of your merit; but as you have often expressed friendship for me, an opportunity presents itself for giving me a proof of it. You are, besides, more a Frenchman than a Spaniard. Shall we have, answer me frankly, the neutrality of Spain, if I undertake anything against the United Provinces?"

"Monsieur," replied Aramis, "the interest of Spain is very clear. To embroil Europe with the United Provinces, against which subsists the ancient malice of their unconquered liberty, is our policy, but the King of France is allied with the United Provinces. You are not ignorant, besides, that it would be a maritime war, and that France is not in a state to make such a one with advantage."

Colbert, turning round at this moment, called d'Artagnan, at the same time saying in a low voice to Aramis, "We may talk with M. d'Artagnan, I suppose?"

"Oh, certainly," replied the ambassador.

"We were saying, M. d'Alméda and I," said Colbert, "that war with the United Provinces would be a maritime war."

"That's evident enough," replied the musketeer.

"It results from all this, my dear Monsieur d'Artagnan, that the king would have a very pretty fleet. Now, you know better than anybody else if the land army is good."

D'Artagnan and Aramis looked at each other, wondering at the mysterious labours this man had effected in a few years. Colbert understood them, and was touched by this best of flatteries.

On the morrow of this day, Aramis, who was setting out for Madrid, to negotiate the neutrality of Spain, came to embrace d'Artagnan at his hotel.

"Let us love each other for four," said d'Artagnan; "we are now but two."

"And you will, perhaps, never see me again, dear d'Artagnan," said Aramis. "If you knew how I have loved you! I am old, I am extinguished, I am dead."

"My friend," said d'Artagnan, "you will live longer than I shall: diplomacy commands you to live; but for my part, honour condemns me to die."

"Bah! Such men as we are, Monsieur le Marshal," said Aramis, "only die satiated with joy or glory."

"Ah!" replied d'Artagnan, with a melancholy smile, "I assure you, Monsieur le Duc, I feel very little appetite for either." They once more embraced, and, two hours after, they were separated.

The Death of D'Artagnan

In the spring, as Colbert had predicted, the land army entered on its campaign. It preceded, in magnificent order, the court of Louis XIV, who, setting out on horseback, surrounded by carriages filled with ladies and courtiers, conducted the *élite* of his kingdom to this sanguinary fête. The officers of the army, it is true, had no other music but the artillery of the Dutch forts; but it was enough for a great number, who found in this war honours, advancement, fortune, or death.

M. d'Artagnan set out commanding a body of twelve thousand men, cavalry and infantry, with which he was ordered to take the different places which form the knots of that strategic network which is called La Frise. Never was an army conducted more gallantly to an expedition. The officers knew that their leader, prudent and skilful as he was brave, would not sacrifice a single man, nor yield an inch of ground without necessity. He had the old habits of war, to live upon the country, keep his soldiers singing and the enemy weeping. The captain of the King's musketeers placed his coquetry in showing that he knew his business. Never were opportunities better chosen, *coups de main* better supported, errors of the besieged taken better advantage of.

The army commanded by d'Artagnan took twelve small places within a month. He was engaged in besieging the thirteenth, which had held out five days. D'Artagnan caused the trenches to be opened without appearing to suppose that these people would ever allow themselves to be taken. The pioneers and labourers were, in the army of this man, a body full of emulation, ideas, and zeal, because he treated them

186

like soldiers, knew how to render their work glorious, and never allowed them to be killed if he could prevent it. It should have been seen then, with what eagerness the marshy glebes of Holland were turned over. Those turf-heaps, those mounds of potter's clay melted at the word of the soldiers like butter in the vast frying-pans of the Friesland house-wives.

M. d'Artagnan dispatched a courier to the King to give him an account of the last successes, which redoubled the good humour of His Majesty and his inclination to amuse the ladies. These victories of M. d'Artagnan gave so much majesty to the Prince, that Madame de Montespan no longer called him anything but Louis the Invincible. So that Mademoiselle de la Vallière, who only called the King Louis the Victorious, lost much of His Majesty's favour. Besides, her eyes were frequently red, and for an Invincible nothing is more disagreeable than a mistress who weeps while everything is smiling around her. The star of Mademoiselle de la Vallière was being drowned in the horizon in clouds and tears. But the gaiety of Madame de Montespan redoubled with the successes of the King, and consoled him for every other unpleasant circumstance. It was to d'Artagnan the King owed this; and His Majesty was anxious to acknowledge these services; he wrote to M. Colbert:—

"Monsieur Colbert, we have a promise to fulfil with M. d'Artagnan, who so well keeps his. This is to inform you that the time is come for performing it. All provisions for this purpose you shall be furnished with in due time.—Louis."

In consequence of this, Colbert, who detained the envoy of d'Artagnan, placed in the hands of that messenger a letter from himself for d'Artagnan, and a small coffer of ebony inlaid with gold, which was not very voluminous in appearance, but which, without doubt, was very heavy, as a guard of five men was given to the messenger, to assist him in carrying it. These people arrived before the place which d'Artagnan was besieging towards daybreak and presented themselves at the lodgings of the general. They were told that M. d'Artagnan, annoyed by a sortie which the governor, an artful man, had made the evening before, and in which the works had been destroyed, seventy-seven men killed, and the reparation of the breaches commenced, had just gone, with half a score companies of grenadiers, to reconstruct the works.

M. Colbert's envoy had orders to go and seek M. d'Artagnan wherever he might be, or at whatever hour of the day or night. He directed his course, therefore, towards the trenches, followed by his escort, all on horseback. They perceived M. d'Artagnan in the open plain with his gold-laced hat, his long cane, and his large gilded cuffs. He was biting his white moustache, and wiping off, with his left hand, the dust which the passing balls threw up from the ground they ploughed near him. They also saw, amidst this terrible fire, which filled the air with its hissing whistle, officers handling the shovel, soldiers rolling barrows, and vast fascines, rising by being either carried or dragged by from ten to twenty men, cover the front of the trench, reopened to the centre by this extraordinary effort of the general animating his soldiers. In three hours, all had been reinstated. D'Artagnan began to speak more mildly; and he became quite calm, when the captain of the pioneers approached him, hat in hand, to tell him that the trench was again lodgeable. This man had scarcely finished speaking when a ball took off one of his legs, and he fell into the arms of d'Artagnan. The latter lifted up his soldier; and quietly, with soothing words, carried him into the trench, amidst the enthusiastic applause of the two regiments. From that time, it was no longer ardour: it was delirium; two companies stole away up to the advanced posts, which they destroyed instantly.

When their comrades, restrained with great difficulty by d'Artagnan, saw them lodged upon the bastions, they rushed forward likewise; and soon a furious assault was made upon the counterscarp, upon which depended the safety of the place. D'Artagnan perceived there was only one means left of stopping his army, and that was to lodge it in the place. He directed all his force to two breaches, which the besieged were busy in repairing. The shock was terrible; eighteen companies took part in it, and d'Artagnan went with the rest, within half cannon-shot of the place, to support the attack by échelons. The cries of the Dutch who were being poniarded upon their guns by d'Artagnan's grenadiers, were distinctly audible. The struggle grew fiercer with the despair of the governor, who disputed his position foot by foot. D'Artagnan, to put an end to the affair, and silence the fire, which was unceasing, sent a fresh column, which penetrated like a wimble through the posts that remained solid; and he soon perceived upon the ramparts, through the fire, the terrified flight of the besieged, pursued by the besiegers.

It was at this moment the general, breathing freely and full of joy, heard a voice behind him, saying, "Monsieur, if you please, from M. Colbert."

He broke the seal of a letter which contained these words:—

"MONSIEUR D'ARTAGNAN,—The King commands me to inform you that he has nominated you Marshal of France, as a reward of your good services, and the honour you do to his arms. The King is highly pleased, monsieur, with the captures you have made; he commands you in particular, to finish the siege you have commenced, with good fortune to you and success for him."

D'Artagnan was standing with a heated countenance and a sparkling eye. He looked up to watch the progress of his troops upon the walls, still enveloped in red and black volumes of smoke. "I have finished," replied he to the messenger; "the city will have surrendered in a quarter of an hour." He then resumed his reading:—

"The accompanying box, Monsieur d'Artagnan, is my own present. You will not be sorry to see that, whilst you warriors are drawing the sword to defend the King, I am animating the pacific arts to ornament the recompenses worthy of you. I commend myself to your friendship, Monsieur le Marshal, and beg you to believe in all mine.

— COLBERT."

D'Artagnan, intoxicated with joy, made a sign to the messenger, who approached, with his box in his hands. But at the moment the marshal was going to look at it, a loud explosion resounded from the ramparts, and called his attention towards the city.

"It is strange," said d'Artagnan, "that I don't see the King's flag upon the walls, or hear the drums beat." He launched three hundred fresh men, under a high-spirited officer, and ordered another breach to be beaten. Then, being more tranquil, he turned towards the box which Colbert's envoy held out to him. It was his treasure, he had won it.

D'Artagnan was holding out his hand to open the box, when a ball from the city crushed the box in the arms of the officer, struck d'Artagnan full in the chest, and knocked him down upon a sloping heap of earth, while the fleur-de-lised baton, escaping from the broken sides of the box, came rolling under the powerless hand of the marshal. D'Artagnan endeavoured to raise himself up. It was thought he had been knocked down without being wounded. A terrible cry broke from the group of his terrified officers; the marshal was covered with blood; the paleness of death ascended slowly to his noble countenance. Leaning upon the arms which were held out on all sides to receive him, he was able once more to turn his eyes towards the place, and to distinguish the white flag at the crest of the principal bastion; his ears, already deaf to the sounds of life, caught feebly the rolling of the drum which announced the victory. Then, clasping in his nerveless hand the baton ornamented with its fleur-de-lis, he cast down upon it his eyes, which had no longer the power of looking upwards towards heaven, and fell back, murmuring those strange words, which appeared to the soldiers cabalistic words,—words which had formerly represented so many things upon earth, and which none but the dying man longer comprehended.

"Athos—Porthos, farewell till we meet again! Aramis, *adieu* for ever!"

Of the four valiant men whose history we have related, there now no longer remained but one single body; God had resumed the souls.

Also available in

CHILDREN'S
CLASSICS

The Call of the Wild

Jack London

Jack London (1876-1916) was born in San Francisco and grew up on the waterfront of Oakland. Much of his youth was spent on the wrong side of the law.

He joined the Klondike gold rush in 1897, returning to Oakland to write about his experiences there.

The Call of The Wild is the story of Buck, half St Bernard, half sheepdog, stolen from his comfortable Californian home and taken to the Klondike as a sled dog.

How Buck learns to endure and to be free is inspiringly told in Jack London's classic story of survival.

Also available in

CHILDREN'S
CLASSICS

Uncle Tom's Cabin

Harriet Beecher Stowe

Harriet Elizabeth Beecher Stowe, authoress of
Uncle Tom's Cabin, was born at Lichfield,
Connecticut, USA, in 1812.

Uncle Tom's Cabin, which is a direct attack
upon the system of slavery that then existed in
the Southern States, was first published in serial
form in 1851–52. It became immediately
famous, was translated into many foreign
languages, and has since been published in
innumerable editions. It did much to form
public opinion in the United States against
slavery, which was ultimately abolished as a
result of the war between the Northern and
Southern States in 1861–65.

Also available in

Treasure Island

R.L. Stevenson

Robert Louis Stevenson (1850-94) was born in Scotland and journeyed widely, from Spain to the California gold-fields, finally settling in Samoa, where he died. By then he was recognized as one of the greatest story tellers ever, and *Treasure Island* has become one of the world's best-loved adventure stories.

The story begins with a mysterious treasure map and an old buccaneer in an English country inn: soon we are on the high seas in a dangerous Caribbean quest that becomes a desperate battle of wits between young Jim Hawkins and the unforgettable wily old pirate Long John Silver.

As the tension mounts, who will be first to find the dead man's chest and its fabulous treasure?

Also available in

CHILDREN'S
CLASSICS

Stories from Andersen

Hans Christian Andersen

The fairy tales of Hans Christian Andersen were first published in English translation in 1846 and have remained firm favourites as bedtime stories ever since.

There are the most familiar tales such as *The Ugly Duckling*, *Thumbykin* and *The Emperor's New Clothes*, which have been told and re-told sometimes in song, dance, theatre or cinema, but here we also have some of the less well-known ones; they too deserve their place in this classic collection. Hans Christian Andersen's fairy tales were written for the children of Denmark, but, full of wisdom and timeless magic, they have an appeal for children the world over.

Also available in

What Katy Did

Susan Coolidge

Susan Coolidge, the pseudonym of Sarah
Chauncy Woolsey (1835-1905), was born in
Cleveland, Ohio, and became a children's writer
and literary critic.

Her easy natural style has made the *Katy*
books and her other stories for girls immensely
popular.

In *What Katy Did*, the high-spirited Katy Carr
finds that growing up can be difficult, but it can
also be fun.

The adventures and mishaps of Katy and her
brothers and sisters are engagingly told in Susan
Coolidge's delightful stories.

Also available in

CHILDREN'S
CLASSICS

Don Quixote

Miguel de Cervantes

For over three centuries, readers all over the
world have been delighted by the adventures of
Don Quixote and his squire Sancho Panza.
  Children too should be introduced to the
Quixotic idea and to the lasting charm, pathos
and humour of Cervantes, contained in a new
paperback volume.

Also available in

CHILDREN'S
CLASSICS

A Christmas Carol & Cricket on the Hearth

Charles Dickens

Charles Dickens, probably the best known and most popular English novelist, was born at Portsmouth in 1812. He suffered many hardships as a child and this probably resulted in him becoming an extremely hard worker for all his life. He published many novels dealing with the wrongs inflicted on children by adults in the 19th century.

 A Christmas Carol was a sensational success when it was first published and he followed it in consecutive years with other Christmas books including *Cricket on the Hearth*, also contained in the same volume.

Also available in

CHILDREN'S
CLASSICS

20,000 Leagues Under The Sea

Jules Verne

Jules Verne (1828–1905) was born in France
and became the world's first great science
fiction writer.

In his *20,000 Leagues Under the Sea*, an
expedition led by Professor Aaronax tries to
track down a sea monster that has been sinking
ships all over the world. Their ship explodes and
suddenly they are on board the 'sea monster',
which turns out to be a submarine called *The
Nautilus*, skippered by the mysterious Captain
Nemo—an Indian Prince who has become the
Robin Hood of the open seas, stealing gold to
help the poor.

Verne's prophetic masterpiece of maritime
adventures has fascinated every generation of
readers since its publication in 1870.